The

Freiderici & Paige

Copyright © 2012 Freiderici & Paige

All rights reserved.

ISBN:147508076X
ISBN-13:978-1475080766

This book is a work of fiction and any resemblance to persons, living or dead, or places, events or locales is purely coincidental. The characters are productions of the author's imagination and used fictitiously.

Young Adult Reading Material

ACKNOWLEDGEMENTS

To Mirinus, thank you for allowing me to use your name. You are more dazzling and beautiful than I could convey and, yes, you are one of my angels.

To all the people (clients/patients) who over the years have confided in me, thank you. Your trust means a lot to me.

To all the people that, in one way or another, have contributed to make us the individuals that we are. Thank you.

CONTENTS

1	After The Fog	11
2	The Meadow	27
3	The Mountain	49
4	Gentle Giants	59
5	The Shelf	69
6	A Happy Accident	81
7	Green Eyes	97
8	The Gifts	115
9	They Moved Stones	129
10	About Tamara, Love and Anger.	155
11	A Little Surprise	163
12	Ulrich's Mistake	177
13	Flying Horses	199

14	They Fly, Sing and The Stone Snake Smiles.	217
15	Ulrich's Fall	231
16	There Is Going To Be A Wedding.	245
17	Sophie Remembers	253
18	Releasing The Past	263
19	The Celebration	271

1

AFTER THE FOG

Sophie stirred, then braced for the attack. Nothing happened. She opened one eye and there was nothing. Neither of the dogs were breathing in her face, eagerly wagging tails, as they had done for years. She sat up on the bed and looked at them.

The girl dog, gave her a one-eye glance. "It's Ok girl... sleep in, if you like." Sophie said.

She got out of bed and petted the blue-heeler. The boy dog remained, stretched as long as he was, on the other side of the bed. *Wow, I didn't think they would be this tired after yesterday's walk. They must be getting old. Poor things.* she thought, as she made her way to the bathroom.

The bathroom light did not come on and Sophie mentally cursed the electric company. *Power must be out. So much for underground utilities.* She relieved herself, flushed the toilet, then proceeded to wash her hands and teeth. The water had been unpleasantly cold. *How long has the power been out?* She would have to unpack the gas burner.

Sophie kept an emergency kit. After an ice storm in this town, anyone would. *Oh no... we are not doing this again...* had been her promise to herself, after being stuck in traffic for hours, during the last snow storm. The prospect of working the gas burner did not appeal to her. It had been over a decade since her last "field" cooking experience.

As she worked her way to the kitchen, her main concern was to try to get information about the power outage. Finally, the dogs followed. They moved slow and uncertain and her heart ached at the prospect of loosing them to old age.

While opening the door to the back deck, she asked them sweetly, "Outside?" They perked-up a little and stepped onto the deck, smelling the air as they descended the steps to the yard. She decided to watch them from the deck. This crazy weather, she thought. It had been freezing the night before but it was mild and cool now. *Very nice, if only there was not so much fog.*

This was the time of the year when the field behind the house turned emerald green. As light came in, her eyes followed the swirls of mist slow dance with the breeze. She never tired of watching the colors go from washed to vivid. There was little faithful, the deer who came to sample from the salt lick every day.

Jessie and Michael had placed the stone just beyond their property line. They loved to watch the deer come by and the salt lick had seemed like a good idea at the time. It really was lovely to see them, except that they came around so often now, that the neighbors had faced more than one close encounter with the beasts.

She remembered the morning a deer had jumped in front of her car. She was just recovering from the near miss and was about to turn left into her driveway, when a driver came from behind and almost hit her. In order to avoid her car, the driver had been forced to turn hard left and go over her flower beds. He had also missed hitting her mailbox by inches. He could have either hit her or the medieval looking thing. Either way would have made for a really bad day. The driver had not stopped, so she reported the incident to the authorities.

Children walked the streets at that time. There were at least six kids who walked by her house, every morning, on their way to the corner school bus stop. Even though, she had an idea that the driver had also been distracted by running deer, she did not excuse his apparent lack of concern. People seemed to be in too much of a hurry these days.

Still smiling at the memory of the commotion that her young neighbors had inadvertently caused, she turned to look at their house and something froze inside of her. Only when her throat began to itch, did she realize that she had stood in place, slacked jaw, staring at an empty lot. Actually, there were trenches where the foundation had been. Were her eyes fooling her? The house was not there! The mist retreated more and there was no mistaking it. The house was not there.

She swirled and stepped forward to check for the other houses, so violently that she almost lost her balance. She clutched at the railing to steady herself. Somewhere, in the back of her mind, she heard her voice screaming, yelling at her to wake up; move! She felt slightly lightheaded and remembered reading something about shallow breathing doing that to people. She forced herself to take a couple of deep, deliberate breaths. There seemed to be less houses. Was she loosing her mind? The house on the other side of hers was also gone.

"Bear! Termite! House!" The beasts sensed the urgency in her voice and responded, immediately, to her command. She slammed shut and locked the back door, then ran to the front door. There was very little past the driveway. *Josh!* her heart did a somersault. "Upstairs!" She commanded the beasts *Dear God, no, not him. Please. Let. Him. Be. There!* she mentally pleaded, as they all three scrambled up the stairs.

Oh my God, what is happening? Sophie silently asked, as she stopped at his bedroom door, holding her breath, afraid to look in. She waited until her eyes adjusted to the darkness, and under the faint light coming through the window, she saw the bundle of her son on his bed. The sound of a soft snore released her breath in relief. His breathing was strong and steady. She took another deep breath and walked to the window, to make sure of what she had seen, before waking him up. Outside, the mist had rolled away quite a bit. There was not mistaking what she knew. The houses around hers, were gone.

"Josh" she said softly. "Wake up sweetie. Something has happened."

"Huh?" came his answer.

"C'mon sweetie... Power's out and something's weird going on."

"What?" He asked as he sat up.

"Josh... Take a deep breath. It looks like the houses out there are gone. I know it sounds crazy but, I swear, I can't see them."

"Mom..." He groaned. "Do you have your glasses?"

"Josh, just humor me and take a look. Please?"

In the semi-darkness, she heard him take a deep breath, get up and out of his bed and grumble: "OK, but let me go to the bathroom first."

"Hum..Ok" she said, absentminded. The images of the empty lots kept on going around and around in her mind. She tried to remember if she had ever heard of anything similar having happened to other people before. *How can anyone sleep through something like this?* She waited outside the upstairs bathroom, for him to finish. Once he was done, they both went downstairs and out the front door.

"Wait... what the..." he swore softly.

They looked around and saw nothing but hills and fields, to the front, side and back of the house. There were trenches, debris, trees and flower beds but structures, lamp posts and cars were gone.

"Are we dreaming Mom?" He turned to her.

"If we are, it would be the first time we would both have the same dream and... this is too... real." she said as she looked around and felt the cold cement of the driveway under her bare feet. She didn't tell him that there had been some houses left, before she went upstairs to get him.

"OK, let's get back in the house and think about this." he said, still trying to wake up. He felt good but found it difficult to think.

"Let's try to see if we can access the Internet through the Blackberry and your smart phone. One of those have to work." she said.

Back inside, they tried both devices but neither could find a network. Without electricity, the wireless would not work, so the laptops were also useless and they could not find their emergency, hand cranked powered, radio.

"The Car!" they said in unison, moving towards the garage. They tried all the stations but there was only static.

"This, is not good." he said, trying to remain calm. "This is like a scifi movie."

Trying to get their minds into practical things, to avoid panic, she began: "Ok, let's forget about the news for a bit. There is still some water in the tank and we have the water gallons for emergencies. We have food and the gas burner, so we will be Ok for a little while." To herself she thought that she would just like to know what happened to the rest of houses and the people. *How can a house disappear just like that?*

"We need to get organized." she continued. "We can't use the bathrooms because we don't know if there is a sewage system left. We will have to make a field latrine; a field bathroom. Dig a hole to go do number two and so on." she explained. Years of Army training coming back to her. "We have potable water but we need to find more. There is the river by the park, remember? It will be a good walk so we will have to be disciplined about how we use our water. We have to gather wood to make a fire to boil water, both for drinking and for cooking."

Josh nodded. Years living with his Mom had taught him to listen and take mental notes. She had taken care of him by herself, during enough years that he had learned to trust this woman. He also knew that this was how she gathered her thoughts. His mother needed to have a plan to feel secure. She needed to talk about what they should do, so that she felt reassured that they could work as a team. She would definitely listen and respect his opinion but, for the time being, she needed to talk.

He was also trying to comprehend what he had just seen. Her chatter, allowed him to retreat into his mind to try to sort things out. This was not the time to panic. They had to take measures to survive and not wait until the water and rations were gone. He also had the urge to build something like a shelter. Actually, it was more like an urge to get out of the house.

They took one last look outside, then began to unpack the gas burner and prepare breakfast. They had enough rice, beans, energy drinks, bottled water and canned tuna and meats to last them for several months. In addition, there were two boxes of dehydrated meals that she had purchased on a whim.

Back when the recession hit, people began to look around to see how the rest of the world was doing. There were news about financial meltdowns, revolutions, natural disasters and crazy weather. After a couple of hours of news shock, even Sophie decided that it was better to be safe than sorry.

She had not felt the need to build a bunker in some far, undisclosed location, like she saw people do in a TV program. However, at this moment, the thought of having those supplies was very comforting. Sophie had read, somewhere, that the average American family would not have enough to eat beyond a couple of weeks, so she had purchased enough to last them several months. She never expected to actually have to use those supplies.

At present, it was the food in the freezer what worried her. If the weather stayed cold they would be able to stretch those supplies, so that they could save the grains and packaged meats for later. Today, they would have eggs, ham and orange juice.

"Things had been disappearing for a while, you know..." He brought her back from her thoughts.

"No, I don't know. What do you mean?" she stopped getting the items out of the fridge and turned to look at him.

"At school, we noticed some people stopped coming to school and nobody could get in touch with them." Sitting at the table, he looked uncertain. He wanted to tell her about the weird things that he had noticed during the past couple of weeks. "Didn't you notice there were less cars on the streets?"

"Yes, but it is spring break. I figured people had left for vacation or that maybe some of the families had moved." She raised both eyebrows. "Wait. You mean to tell me that you have noticed things and people going away for several weeks now?"

He nodded. "When me and the guys went to visit Alexandra, last time, she said that Lizzie and her family were gone. She said that they called her but the recording said that it was not a working number." He looked as someone who struggled to find the right words. "The same thing happened with Kayla and a couple of the other kids in school." he said carefully. "Even teachers left. Mr. Sanders walked around looking worried. I asked him if he knew where Mr. Miller went and all he said was that he was no longer there. That man did not know what to tell me. I didn't see him anymore. It was pretty quiet at school."

She had been busy for weeks, with clients and projects. She had noticed less people making comments in the social network but she had figured that people were busy, like her. The last four years, she had become a very independent person who never called people, unless there was a real need. Most of the time, she found the phone calls from friends, almost an intrusion. They never seemed to have anything good to say about other people and she had grown to hate gossip. Setting a small frying pan with a dab of olive oil, over the burner she prompted: "Did you notice anything else, Josh?"

"Yes, remember the construction vehicles where they were building that new grocery store? They were gone. Before, I thought I was loosing my mind, so I didn't say anything, but I could have sworn there were a couple of houses missing on Tranton Road."

"Yeah, now that you mention it, I don't remember seeing any of those big, yellow construction vehicles for a while now, either at the market construction site or even here, behind the house. It did look like construction had stopped in the new part of the sub."

The smell of the ham brought her back to the moment. They fixed eggs, ham and cheese burritos for themselves and fed the dogs their food. She boiled water for tea and Josh had some of the orange juice from the fridge. They saved the energy drinks and the bottled water for later.

They ate in silence, looking out through the french doors, at the expanse of green behind their house. It was unsettling to see empty spaces where structures had been. There used to be a water a tower past the corn field; there was only space now.

"We should build a shelter, Mom." he said, finally.

"Why? We have a good shelter right here in this house."

"Well, if the other houses are gone, what is to say that this one will stay?"

"I see what you mean, Josh. But we are here... Where is everybody else? I mean, we are here for a reason. No?"

"Maybe we should walk around and take a closer look at the places where the houses were, Mom."

"OK, let's finish up and get ready. Maybe we can get some answers. I mean, we are good in terms of food. The only thing that could be a problem is... if there is other people around and they have lost their minds. The average person would freak at waking up to something like this."

"How come we are not freaking out?"

"I am not sure. Perhaps because we have lived in between worlds for a while now, remember? We used to talk about this."

"You mean about the change and the things that were going on in the world?"

Sophie nodded, remembering all that she had read about the end of times. There had been so many prophets of doom, as she had liked to call them. One in particular, who talked about dimensional shifts, came to her mind now. She shook her head. Nothing like waking up to something like this, to make one stop and reconsider.

"Yes. Actually, it is a good idea to take a closer look at those sites. According to what I read, only natural, organic or mineral materials would make the change. That would mean that you are right – most of the materials in this house would not stay."

She ran a mental inventory of their belongings and realized that very little would make it through the change. There was either plastic or manufactured metal in everything they had. Even wood was not truly wood because it had the synthetic finishes.

They finished their burritos and washed the dishes with boiling water, from the pan she had set when they sat down to eat. She would have to boil a lot of water in the days to come. She poured the rest of the clean water into a thermos, to keep warm for later use.

They had washed and changed earlier. Now, it was time to venture outside again. She did not wish to leave the familiar environment of her home. She did not wish to learn anymore. She wished she could go back to sleep and wake up in her old life again, but there were still there for a reason.

"Ready?" Her son brought her thoughts back to the moment. The kid was determined to explore and she knew that he had a reason, other than curiosity. He clearly felt the need to leave the house and built a different type of shelter. She also felt that the house would not remain. She just did not want to loose her memories. Loosing the photographs and mementos, that froze in time memories of laughter and discovery with her son, would be like loosing a bit of his childhood.

"Yep. Bear, Termite, outside!" She opened the door for the dogs to lead. "Here, use this to cover your nose and mouth." she said handing him a moistened strip of cloth. "It is dusty out and I have a hunch that there is more than just dirt in that dust. I have the feeling that synthetic materials were reduced to their basic components, which would mean that there is sand and more minerals than usual in that dust. It could irritate our throats." He smiled and did as told. *My Mom... forever the medic,* he thought.

Once outside, they went to the lot next to theirs where Jessie's house once stood. There were deep trenches, pieces of wood and gravel instead of house. She noticed nail holes in several of the pieces. There was also a light dust over the whole area.

"Josh... If the nails that held the poles together disappeared, the walls and roof would come crashing down. We would end up with a pile of wood like this. No?"

"It sounds likely but there is not enough wood here to account for what goes into a house. What happened to rest of it?" Josh remarked.

"I am not sure, sweetie... and what is all this dust? It is a different color from the dirt around here. So, it is a natural material, just not from here?"

There was another material on the ground. She picked a piece. "These fibers are like paper, Josh." She looked around and noticed there was, also, paper litter flying all over the place.

They walked up the hill on what used to be the street. The scene repeated itself in lot after lot. They continued walking and reached the top of the hill. Alexandra's house was not there. The kids used to get together at her place to play games. He stood there in silence staring at the empty lot.

Standing at the top the hill, facing what had been their street, they realized the extent of the devastation. Where houses once stood, they could see miles of empty lots. There were only deep trenches and debris, framed by manicured patches of lawn.

"Let's go back. We could take the car to see if we can find someone else..." she offered.

They could not help but remember the residents as they walked past the lots where their houses once stood. There was the sugar maple Lee planted. There was the small forest of pear trees in bloom that belonged to the lady who used to work on her yard for hours. There was Adam's yard, weed infested and nearly overgrown as always. Across the street from his yard was Jessie's perfect lawn and beautiful rose bushes. The big house, that once had a pool, belonged to Dakota, his brothers and his parents. Jose's house; the boy who, every morning, smiled and waved at her from the school bus stop. His mother had worked at the nearby hospital. A pretty lady with a husband who had given her mean looks, until he realized that she was a neighbor. There was Tyree's house with the leaning tree. Every year they had expected that tree to finally fall and every year, it had made it through the winter. He had been an assistant preacher who raised his family to go to church every Sunday.

These had all been good people. She had loved to see the street come to life in the spring with kids playing on the sidewalks and the neighbors working on their yards. They had been good neighbors. They all had been polite and friendly. They had maintained their yards and created beautiful places to live. Mostly working couples with busy schedules, they had known of each other but socialized briefly. She had been the only one who could have enjoyed more spare time but, then again, working from home had kept her busy. She looked past their street to where the sub had continued. They had known people in those areas also. So many people with whom they had hardly ever socialized. So many people she had liked but never took the time to get know better.

Even though, he had socialized more than his mother, Josh also felt that he could have spent more time with his friends and people that he liked. He had loved to watch little Parker grow from a baby to a commanding three year old. Josh had explored the area and learned all the corners of his neighborhood. This had been home.

Nearing their own yard, they noticed how the sky had darkened. The wind came without warning and lifted a curtain of dust. She yelled at Josh to get into the house then, she turned back, to look at the storm. In the back of her mind, Wagner's Flight of The Valkyries played and She fought the insane urge to giggle. Then, she noticed large objects being carried by the wind.

They had just enough time to exchange looks and bolt for the hallway, where they covered themselves and the dogs with blankets and huddled together on the floor. There were loud knocks, wailing and something like glass shattering. The house shook once and they felt themselves weighted down. It was almost as if the whole house had been lifted.

She put her arm around her son and almost covered him with her body. *Dear God, please protect my son,* she silently prayed. The dogs whimpered and grabbed at them with their claws.

The wind wailed louder and she heard him call: "Mom?"

"I'm here Josh." she answered as calm as she could. She felt lighter but she could still feel her son beside her. "Close your eyes Josh. I have mine closed." She didn't want debris to hurt their eyes.

The floor began to fall away from under them but, somehow, they held on to each other and the dogs. The wind whipped the blankets off but there were no more knocks. When her ears popped, she opened her eyes a squint. There was mist, her son and both dogs. She held on to the female while her son held on to both, the boy dog and her.

He blinked a couple of times and looked at her. There were clouds around them while darkness and lighting below them. She felt lightheaded and drowsy. The dogs had ceased to struggle. *The air is thin up here,* she thought. Her son said something but no sound came out of his mouth, then she faded into darkness.

2
THE MEADOW

She woke up under a blue sky and inhaled deeply. Surprised, she realized that she could almost taste the air. Fresh air tastes like mints; it is crisp and clean. There was the scent of pine and something else, sweet. Instinctively, she turned her head to her right and let out a sigh of relief. There, by her side, lay her son. He was dressed in a rough cotton shirt and trousers. His face, thinner than she remembered, looked peaceful.

Sophie raised herself on one elbow and took account of their surroundings. Turning back to her son, she noticed that he had good color on his cheeks and that his respiration was clear, deep and rhythmic. Slowly, she sat up.

They laid on top of a cotton tarp, in the middle of a meadow. They both wore rough cotton shirt, trousers and leather sandals. There were wooden trunks to their right and piles of rocks all over the place. He took a deep breath, stretched and opened his eyes. He looked at her and blinked a couple of times.

"Mom?"

"Yes, sweetie. I'm here."

He sat up with a jolt and looked around. Realization dawning on him. This was not a dream. "Man... Where?" He looked around and turned back to her, his eyes asking what he did not dare say aloud.

"I don't know, sweetie. I just got up myself."

His beautiful face looked more mature but still boyish. He touched his shirt, feeling the texture, then looked at his sandals. She smiled at the memory of how hard it had always been to find shoes for his large feet. Well, there he was now, with custom sandals. He looked good, healthy and he was there, with her. She felt relief to see that they had not been separated.

"Mom, are we alive?"

She felt a deep stab of pain at the possibility. *Not my child*, she thought. He was so young. He had not lived. "Josh, this feels real. Can you remember anything?"

"Hum, not much. The storm... the neighbor's houses missing... darkness... I do have a bunch of images but they don't make sense."

"OK, according to what I see, the sun is almost above, so it is either near or just after lunch. At any rate, we may not have many hours of daylight left." she said. She snickered at herself, realizing that she had switched to her 'practical mode' in order to avoid fear. "We should look around, gather wood and try to figure out how to set up a camp. Let's see what's in those trunks. Let's hope there's some food."

Josh nodded. Last time they woke up to a crazy situation, at least they got the chance to have breakfast. *Let's hope we don't get... whatever happened before*, he thought.

Little by little clarity began to come back to her. It was her and her son now, standing in the middle of a meadow. There were piles of stones and boulders everywhere. *These stones did not occur naturally.* They had been placed in piles at certain intervals. There were wooden boxes piled to their right and, in the distance, they could see animals.

Sophie was certain that they had been plucked off the earth and preserved somehow. *Just before the house disintegrated...* She remembered covering herself, her son and the dogs with a thick quilt. They had taken shelter in the hallway, under the quilt, to wait out the storm. *The dogs...* At a distance, she saw two shapes.

"Josh, look..." She pointed towards the shapes.

Josh turned and followed her finger. "What? Wait... that looks like Bear and Termite!" he exclaimed.

The shapes moved towards them, then disappeared behind a bush. When they emerged on the other side, it was clear that it was the two dogs. Bear, the heavy one, slipped as he tried to make the curve around one of the piles of stones. Termite, long legged and athletic, did not miss a step.

The boy and his mom grinned as they watched the dogs gallop towards them. Chickens flapped out of the way, while goats and other animals merely glanced and stepped away from the barking dogs.

Cry barking, their whole bodies wagging, the dogs practically threw themselves at their masters. They jumped of joy and tried to reach their master's faces to lick them. The boy leaned over and hugged the big, black male while the mother tried to soothe the female dog. Never had the female been away from her family and she was very vocal and animated. Perhaps, happy, perhaps scolding them, nevertheless, excited at being able to be with them again.

The boy and his mother petted and hugged the beasts. Tears welled in relief and delayed shock. Their lives had changed. They had clearly been taken away from their previous environment and preserved. Whatever had happened, they could get together with other survivors and work to make a new life.

There has to be others. She felt an irrational sense of urgency about getting ready for others. There were the piles of rocks that looked as if something had to be done about them. Several of these rocks were huge and unless she had developed super powers, she had no idea how she was going to move them. There were also the wooden trunks that had been left near for a reason.

Once the dogs calmed down, she motioned for her son to help her with the trunks. They picked the closest one and proceeded to inspect it. It was a simple pine chest with metal hinges and a latch. The latch was unlocked so, they lifted the lid. Inside they were hardly surprised to find bags, utensils and tools. There was a camping ax, pots and pans, a shovel and cooking utensils. There were also canteens, plates and cups. The bags had beans, rice and something like dehydrated meat. This trunk had more than enough for them to set up a kitchen.

"Let's hope there is something to build a shelter in the other trunks." she said.

They must have spent a good hour inspecting the contents of the trunks because, now, the sun was straight overhead. It had been morning and now, it was noon. There was a cool breeze, so it had to be late spring or early summer. She calculated that they had, at most, six hours of daylight left. Sophie turned to Josh and asked: "Josh, please go get us some wood to set up a cooking fire. Be careful about where you step because, even though, we haven't seen any, there could be snakes."

While the boy went to gather wood, followed by his buddy, she began to clear areas for a fire and a shelter. She found large cotton tarps in one of the trunks. If they gathered long, skinny trunks, they could put together an Indian style tepee. Termite, forever the guardian, jumped on top of one of the boulders and set watch over them.

That dog never rests. she smiled to herself. She was glad that the animals had been kept with them. It would be much easier to focus on the task at hand, knowing that their loyal canines were on the watch. Should there be intruders, it wouldn't take much for them to sound the alarm and that was good.

She picked a large ax and waited for Josh to join her. Josh dumped a hefty pile of branches near the trunks. Standing side by side, they scanned the area. There were plenty of saplings, not too far from where they stood.

"I'd like to find tree trunks to build an Indian tepee style shelter for tonight, Josh" she volunteered. "It would be nice if they are slim and tall because slim trees would be easier to cut and carry. Tall so that we can have plenty of head room."

There were plenty of pines around. The saplings near the camp, however, where too soft. They proceeded to the woods. As they got closer, Josh said, "Hey Mom, look. Couldn't we use those for the tepee?"

Following his gaze her eyes rested on a pile of long, slim trunks. *Oh wow, how could I miss that?* she frowned, surprised to see the type of trunks she had just described. "Those are perfect Josh! Good thing, because I was not looking forward having to hack down a tree."

Encouraged that their task had just become much easier, they began to carry the logs back to the camp. Even though, the logs were not heavy, their length made it cumbersome for her to carry. She managed a log while Josh, the show off, carried two; one on each shoulder.

"Boy, don't hurt yourself. We don't have doctors here yet. OK?" she mock scolded him.

Josh just smiled; "OK, Mom." He felt good. He felt stronger than ever. He felt strangely good.

Two more trips and they had enough poles to begin putting the structure of a tepee together. They tied one end of the logs together, with leather strips they found in a trunk, then pushed the other ends into the dirt. Leaning the poles at angles tightened the strips that held them in place. Finally, they covered the logs with thick canvas tarps. It was a simple but stable contraption.

Inside the tepee, it was big enough for them to stretch comfortably at opposite sides, which left the center open for a small fire pit. The hole at the top would provide an escape for the smoke. There was even room for a couple of the trunks, so they dragged inside, the one with the bags of grain and the one with kitchen utensils. They placed them at either side of the entrance. Sophie preferred to keep traffic dirt away from their sleeping areas.

There were still poles left in the pile by the woods, so they also brought those to the camp. They placed four on top of a set of boulders and created a small cove for the other trunks. They built the back side of the cove with stones then, placed stones on the lids of the trunks. If anybody tried to open then, while they slept, that would make enough noise to wake up the dogs. Once the dogs were alerted, they would not stop barking until the intruder was gone. Hopefully, there were no bears around.

They gathered rocks and created a small circle, in the middle of the tepee. Josh brought several sticks for the little fire pit. It would be enough to keep them warm, if needed. There were more tarps and a couple of blankets. She placed a blanket on a tarp for Josh, then decided to place hers at an angle, so that her head would lie near his. The mother instinct never stops looking to protect her children. This way, she could communicate with him without having to raise her voice, should she hear noises outside of the shelter at night.

There was still plenty of daylight, so they went to get more wood. They built another fire pit, outside of the tent. Next, they went to the nearby river and collected water, for boiling, in large pails. Sparks from striking a dark gray rock against the hunting knife, a bundle of dry pine needles, cedar wood shavings and a little patience was all they needed to get the fire going. Once the water had been purified and saved in canteens, she put a small pot of beans to boil. She would add the rice, when the beans were nearly done.

"It's rice and beans tonight, sweetie." she told her son, apologetically. "I'm not ready to try and catch one of those chickens yet."

"That's Ok, Mom. I'm really not that hungry but I know we have to eat." Josh said, smiling at the mental image of his Mom chasing a chicken.

Sophie nodded. "Yes, we do. A lot has happened to us and we need to keep our strength. I'm not that hungry either. We'll see..."

She went back inside and cut a piece of the dehydrated meat and tasted it. *Not bad.* She went back outside and dropped a couple of pieces into the pot with the beans. Looking around, she noticed the dogs. It would take more than a handful of rice and beans to satisfy them. She would have to hunt after all. As if reading her mind, and wishing to spare her the experience, the dogs went to hunt for themselves.

Termite was the best. She was fast and merciless but she did have to wrestle with her catch. Bear got his dinner by virtue of his size, it seemed. The dog ran into a group of ducks and just snapped at the first set of wings that came near his jaws. Once in his maw, it was all over for the duck. Both dogs came back, proudly holding their catch and their tails high.

Good thing I set that other pail with water to boil, she thought. The animals surrendered their catch. Termite did so easily; Bear was not so sure.

Sophie talked little to him: "C'mon big guy... you can't eat raw poultry. It can make you sick and I don't have meds for you..."

The rottweiler, lab mix moved his head away and held on to his catch. He loved his mistress but...

"I promise I only want to clean and cook it for you, OK?" she said, as she gently pried the bird off his jaw.

Good thing this animal loves me, she thought, then wondered if indeed there were that many parasites left on this place. The air was crisp clean and so was the water. All the animals looked healthy. Their coats were full and even; feathers looked shiny and clean... Still, she wasn't going to take any chances.

She placed the birds over a flat rock and proceeded to pour water over them. The bird's skin released the feathers easily, as the boiling water touched it. Very few feathers needed plucking. Josh went to fetch more water for boiling while she opened the birds and looked for the gall bladder. She found the small greenish gland and threw it into the fire.

"Wouldn't want the dogs to get sick." She told Josh. She also found the gizzard and emptied the contents. "Birds' gizzards have stones and undigested food... I'm not sure that it would be good for the dogs to eat that stuff, so I'm not taking any chances." She explained.

As if knowing what she was doing, the dogs watched her movements and waited. That was new. Never had her dogs waited patiently before.

"Can you believe that?" she asked her son, nodding towards the dogs.

Josh smiled at the animals and said: "Nope. They are so good now. I mean, they were always good dogs but now they are... patient."

She finished cleaning the birds and asked her son if he wanted any, to which he answered, "No, not today. Next time. let's feed the dogs."

She had already given them the cleaned and boiled innards so, she stripped as much meat off the bones as she could and boiled it. She threw the bones into the fire so that the dogs could not eat them.

Sophie tore a piece of cloth, about the size of two pillow cases together, and bundled the feathers with it. She told herself that she might as well begin to collect the feathers now. She planned to boil and wash the feathers to use as filling for blankets, pillows and bedding. Next, they found stoneware bowls and washed them with boiling water. She had tossed a couple of handfuls of rice into the beans and now the mixture bubbled nicely.

"The salted meat and wild onions will add flavor and a squeeze of lemon will help in our digestion." She explained to the boy.

The water in the canteens had cooled so they had clean water to drink. They each sat down with a bowl of rice and beans by the fire, while the dogs scarfed their boiled duck. After dinner, they washed the plates with boiling water and sat by the fire to watch the sun set. There was not much to say, this first evening. What does one say in such circumstances?

They left the outside fire burning. Sophie picked a stick from it and brought it inside the tent. With it, she lighted a couple of reeds she had previously left soaking in duck fat.

"I was wondering why you did that Mom..." he commented, as he settled into his sleeping area.

"You mean soak the reeds in fat? I read somewhere that these things were used in place of candles... back in the colonial days." she said, carefully working her way to the middle of the tepee.

"Colonial days..." he repeated then, he added: "No more U.S., huh?"

Sophie glanced at her son. He looked pensive. "We can't say yet, Josh. If we had an airplane, we could fly and take in the big picture. All we know is what we have here." She placed the lighted reed inside the little fire pit and sat down to watch the glow.

"I was just thinking that it might be a good idea to look for higher ground tomorrow." Sophie said, "I mean, if we are going to build permanent shelter, I would like it to be where I can see far in the distance. I would also like to get a little further from the water in case of floods. We don't know how much it rains around here but if we judge by how green and healthy all the plants are, I'd say that these areas have not seen a drought. Also, most of the soil is dark. Do you remember reading about river deltas and the type of soil they had?"

"Very rich and dark...?" he winked.

"Correct." she smiled back. "I think we are in an area that gets flooded, not a delta of course, but wet enough that sediments from up river enrich the clay soil."

Both dogs found spots near the entrance and settled in for the night. Tonight, they would camp here. As soon as she could, however, she would look for higher ground. Back in their old life, news of floods had become almost commonplace.

"Here we have a small camp and food enough for several days. Soon we will have to think about building a stronger shelter and hunting to have food for the winter." Sophie said.

Laying on his back, Josh remembered winter in the old house. "You're thinking of snow?"

Sophie took a minute to remember their surroundings. "There are pine trees and no tropical vegetation. Josh, I think this place gets winter snow. I looks very similar to our place and we used to get snow. I think it would be better to plan for the future."

"OK. That means that we have to make some kind of place for those chickens out there, so we can get their eggs." he said "Something like a chicken coop." Then he asked: "Are you thinking about building a log house?"

"Yes, there are plenty or rocks around that we could use for the foundation and, hopefully, we will find logs bigger than these." she said looking up at the structure. "If push comes to shove, the Indians survived winter in these structures. We could make some more and cover them with animal skins."

He shook his head. "I much rather have a real house, Mom. It would suck to have go outside in the winter, to go to the bathroom."

She laughed out loud "No kidding! We didn't even want to walk the dogs during winter, back in the old house, remember?"

He did. He felt a stab of pain at the thought of his previous life and all that had been left behind. He was thankful to be alive and all, but the future was so uncertain... "Mom, do you think that whoever placed us here will show up to talk to us?" he asked.

She caught his meaning immediately "I hope so. Look, we know that we were kept healthy. I caught my reflection on the water and I could swear I look younger. I look at my hands and the skin looks younger."

Josh smiled. "You do look younger Mom."

"See... these people did something to us; to preserve us. They will want to see how things go but I wouldn't sit around waiting for them. I think we need to get ourselves settled as best we can. There are animals, a source of water, wood and rocks. We have several bags of grains, which are basically seeds, and tools. Everything tells me that we are meant to build."

"To prepare for the others?" he asked uncertainly.

"You can also feel it?" she turned to look at him.

"Yes. I can't explain how I know but I know that others will come." then he grinned: "If you build it, they will come, remember?"

She laughed and shook her head. "Yep. That was a classic." Her son may have been over 6 feet tall but she knew he was just a kid. He was taking this experience very well. Grown men would have lost their minds already. In spite of the humor, she knew the boy was making an effort to keep from burdening her with his fears. "Thank you sweetie" she said.

Nearly asleep, Josh mumbled: "Hum? For what?"

"For being such a trooper." she finished.

Sophie reached over to ruffle her son's hair, then laid down on her back. She thought about all they had been through. The idea that someone had taken them off their house, *while the thing disintegrated,* was overwhelming. Then, they had been left here, *with supplies and tools but no message; no instructions... nothing.* She had read so many theories but never experienced anything ~this~ paranormal. She fell asleep, tortured by questions.

Sophie had dreams. In one of her dreams, she opened her eyes to a glare. At the time, she thought of the sun and the stars. There was somebody else there with her. It did not feel like anyone she had met before but it was, somehow, familiar and comforting. She laid on a white surface. It was not a bed but it was not a table either. She turned her head and met clear green eyes. There were lights behind that face. There must have been lights because that face had a glow. She remembered feeling very drowsy and heavy so that she could not move much. Her fingers told her that she laid on something soft but not silk. It felt as if she went in and out of consciousness several times.

Next, she found herself back in the world as it was, floating above it. She witnessed riots where people were extremely violent to each other. Police, in military gear, threw gas grenades and bashed people's skulls with their sticks. People responded by throwing rocks and Molotovs. She watched, in horror, as the bottles hit the pavement and splashed those around. Fire jumped and latched onto their legs and people ran, screaming in pain. She saw faces bloodied and distorted. There were bodies on the ground and lots of broken glass and debris. She closed her eyes and turned her head.

She felt a presence beside her and turned. There were those green eyes again. "You have to look." A deep masculine voice, with a thick accent, said. She had heard that voice before. His eyes were stern but not unkind. She turned her face to the left and faced the scene below her.

There were dead bodies floating in dirty water. Children splashed and played nearby. Adults yelled at the children to get out of the water and when the kids did not obey, they went in to get them. The adults carried the children for miles, away from the bodies, until the procession reached a mountain. As the people stepped out of the water, the skin on their legs and feet looked macerated. They had sores, and places where the skin had sloughed off. It was repugnant to see flies lay eggs on the raw red skin. Larvae grew out and some fell on the ground; some became flies and some went into their brains.

Sophie went higher and saw the whole world. There were gold threads above the earth. People on earth could not see them from below but many knew of their existence. In many places, people had reached and tied their precious things with that thread. There were other people who wanted to take the threads away. They built huge towers to grab at the gold and keep it for themselves. When the people complained, they built walls to surround the people. Since the people could not see outside, they believed what the owners told them.

Next, Sophie found herself riding on a motorcycle. There was another rider beside her. He gave her a wonderful smile and nodded towards a bridge. They both took the bridge to go around the walls but as they approached, storm clouds gathered. He continued to smile and so did she. She could practically smell the negative ions in the storm. She felt exhilarated as her bike took off the ground. There were huge clouds and long bolts of thunder. Her bike fell off but she continued to soar. She felt free and happy.

Fearless, she descended on a strange street. People peeked behind curtains in all the houses. She reached and touched a fence and was able to feel the roughness of the stone. Men, by cars, called to her. They would love to take her with them. She smiled and said: "No thank you. Maybe later." It felt strange to speak of death so casually.

She saw a crowd behind a glass. They became alarmed when they saw her. They began to speak fast; too fast to make any of the words. They looked like human machines. She wanted to help them but they could not hear her. "It is only a dream" she said. Sadly, she turned and walked away.

She woke up sad. *That was a crazy dream*, she thought. Nevertheless, she was here now and there was much to do. She turned to check on her son and saw that he was not there. Apprehension grappled at her throat but she pushed it back down. *Enough!* she told herself. *He is six feet tall and almost two hundred pounds. We had been protected, preserved and gently placed in a peaceful area with supplies. We are going to be OK!*

She ran her fingers through her hair and wished she had a mirror. She may look younger but she was sure that by now her hair, probably, looked very similar to something like a chicken's nest. She ripped a thin length of canvas and used part of it to tie her hair into a pony tail. *That will have to do. At least it's off my face.* Grabbing the small shovel from the trunk she went outside the tent.

"Good morning Mom! Look what I got!" Josh beamed at her from beside the fire pit and pointed towards a bowl on the ground.

Surprised, Sophie joined him. "Eggs! How did you get those? I thought the chickens wouldn't let anyone near."

"Yeah, it was tricky… I got up very early, actually, the Termite and Bear woke me up super early and we went out exploring." He looked at her to see if she was upset. She wasn't, so he continued, "I think the chickens were asleep. The dogs were amazing… they didn't scare them or anything; just pointed me to where they were." He was clearly pleased with the dogs and the results of their little expedition. "Did you know that chickens snore?" he added, as he prepared the fire.

Sophie picked one of the eggs. "Did you check these eggs against the light sweetie?"

"Yes Ma'am... I remembered what you told me about fertilized eggs. These didn't have any shadows inside." he nodded firmly.

One by one, she held each against the sun. The boy was right; there were, indeed, no shadows inside. "You're right. You did good Josh." she beamed at him then asked: "So, what are we having?"

"Scrambled." he said. "Sunny side up takes too much oil, plus I'm not sure about this pan."

"These are actually very good." she said, picking up one of the heavy pans. "It reminds me of cast iron pans. Back in the day, we used to season them by cooking onions in oil, until darkened."

Remembering the stories his mother had told him, Josh commented: "That's right. Seasoning was so that food wouldn't stick to them, right?"

"That's right..." Thinking about all that she had learned from her grandmother, she went to relieve and wash herself by the river. It wasn't a long walk. The Termite ran around her, so that Sophie felt confident that any critters had cleared the area. Once back at the camp, she sat down by the fire and gave Josh a comical frown. "What were you saying about snoring chickens?"

Joshua grinned and said: "I'm telling you... they made this weird little sound..."

"I think that was called cooing..." Sophie mock corrected her son.

"OK, but I prefer to say they snore." Josh enjoyed the easy banter with his Mom. He smiled as he placed the pan back on the fire. He had removed it so that the oil wouldn't burn, waiting for his Mom to come back. Nobody likes cold eggs. Once the oil looked fluid, he cracked the eggs into the pan and threw the shells at the dogs, who laid down to lick the insides. The dogs had caught a rabbit earlier and ate it but he didn't think it was a good time to tell his Mom. There was nothing, really, that could be done until they had a place with a fence... *at least a door.*

Sophie shared a little of her scrambled eggs with the dogs. "They haven't beg as they used to..." she commented. "Guess they're still full from last night's duck..."

Josh just looked at the dogs, "Uhum."

She forgot about the dogs and focused on the day ahead. "We probably have enough protein to hold us until lunch, but we should try to find greens and fruit to add carbs to our diet." Today, she decided, they would explore their surroundings. "Josh, we should pack some water and plan to explore around here. We may want to bring the knife, the machete and a piece of the tarp in case we find food to carry back."

"We can also look for a better place to build, Mom." Josh reminded her.

She nodded. "That's right. We need to find a better place."

"So, where should we start?" He asked, taking the cleaned pots and dishes back inside the tent.

She studied their surroundings and noticed an upward slope, from the wood line behind their tent. She also noticed that the piles of rocks, which she had assumed to be all over the place, actually made a line toward the same slope. "Well, it looks like those rocks are marking the way, Josh. What do you think?"

"Might as well follow them, Mom." He handed her the knife and kept the machete for himself.

In addition to the knife, Sophie brought a piece of tarp. She hoped to find fruit and greens to add to their menu. She would tie the tarp behind her neck and collect her finds in the fold. The tarp would make a good wrap around carrier.

"I think we are set Mom." Josh said.

3

THE MOUNTAIN

Conifers, as well as, deciduous trees shaded the path. Most of the tree trunks were about a foot across, which told her that this was probably not an old forest. It was an easy climb. The dogs ran ahead and back to them, happy to go for a walk. They had always loved to go to the park, near their old house.

Dogs develop relationships with humans, similar to packs. For a dog, to go out for a walk in the woods with its family, is the ultimate bonding experience. The dogs barreled through bushes in chase of small critters. They busted out of the woods and back into the path with goofy hanging tongues and wild eyes. Sophie and her son walked slowly but with purpose. They loved watching the dogs' happy antics. From time to time, they stopped to take in their surroundings.

"Do you hear that?" He asked.

She paused and what she had thought was wind, came clearly as the sound of rushing water. "Yes, it sounds like water..."

They followed the stones to another clearing. There, they found a small lake fed by a waterfall. She stopped to admire the scene. Fine gravel lined the shores and the water was so clear that they could see fish swimming. Beyond, boulders and stones captured the rushing water into pools. Moss, growing on the boulders, could be seen through clear sheets of water. Ferns, growing in crevices, stretched out of bounds seeking the light. Cherry and Willow trees, with outstretched branches, framed the scene and behind the clearing, stood the mountains. It was an enchanted place.

The piles of stones continued up the hill to their right, so they decided to follow. Something urged them to follow. The trail turned left, then right again and, finally, they were rewarded with an amazing space. They had found a huge shelf in the mountain that created a clearing. From this vantage point, they could see miles in either direction. There was the path they had followed, the meadows and the river beyond. The lake rested slightly below, off to their right. Not much of it could be seen from where they stood. The lake, however, was close enough that a short walk would provide for their needs. Behind them, stood higher mountains. This might be a good place to build a home.

"Mom!" Josh called, excited. "Come and take a look at this!"

"What is it?" she turned and hurried in his direction.

"You are not going to believe this. We have an orchard!" he yelled back.

An orchard... exactly what I had been wishing for... Somehow, she was not surprised. She had sat on a rock to enjoy the view, while he had gone off to explore the surroundings with his buddy. Now, Josh guided her through a path, in between maples, on to a higher clearing, where there were short, fat trees. He was right; there were fruit trees.

"These remind me of the pear tree we had on the front yard." she said, touching one of the branches, loaded with fat little green bulbs. "These other ones, are a little different so I'm going to venture that they could be apple trees." She had wished for apples, pears and cherries.

"Wouldn't it be nice if we also found peanuts... hazelnuts... walnuts... strawberries and blueberries?" she wished aloud, pausing at each name to recall the image, smell and flavor of each fruit, just in case...

"We just might, Mom. This place is, so far, amazing. Isn't it?" Josh said, delighted.

"Yes, it is..." she said, looking around and taking in the beauty. "The weather has been perfect. I didn't feel any bugs, down by the river and everything is so lush and healthy."

Josh thought a moment. This could not be earth. "It feels better than earth, Mom."

"It sort of does..." she felt that they were still on earth but could not argue against her son's idea. This place did feel better than earth. Perhaps it was the true blue sky. She had seen photos of other places on earth, just as beautiful; far away places, unspoiled by tourists. She had loved her home but, she had to admit that neither the sky nor the plants *ever looked so... clean.* "Anyhow... we should be able to harvest the fruit from these trees in about three months. It would be nice to find berries because they produce earlier. Let's see if we can find any berry bushes."

The orchard continued around the hill until they found more large stones. The stones created a natural path of steps which they climbed to another clearing and there they were... Strawberries growing in the crevices of stones. There were bushes that, she was almost certain, would produce peanuts and hazelnuts. *We will, probably, find blueberry bushes back near the river.*

They stood and stared at the strawberries. They felt happiness and apprehension, at the same time. "It is not too good to be true. There is something about this place that works this way, Josh." she voiced his thoughts.

"I know..." he said quietly.

"Thoughts and words become things." she repeated something she had heard a very long time.

"That is good. Isn't it?" he asked.

"It is good." she confirmed. There had to be more to it, though. It couldn't be that simple. Something told her that it was not as simple as wishing aloud.

"OK... let's just pick some to eat. I'd like to go back to the big clearing and talk about the house." Josh said, taking charge of the moment.

"Hum.. huh. Sure." she said, absentmindedly, and moved to pick the juiciest, reddest strawberries she had ever seen.
On the way back to the clearing, she bent over a bright green puff of grass and cut a couple of blades. "This smells like lemon grass. I'm going to try to make some tea later." she said, stuffing the cuts inside the bundle. They picked a flat boulder and sat.

"What type of house are we talking about Mom? A log house?" he asked, while munching on a strawberry.

"It seems like the thing to do. We would need to build a stone foundation to keep the logs off the ground. Moisture can rot the wood and bring termites."

"More than the one we already have?" he joked.

"I know... that dog..." she rolled her eyes.

The Termite got her name because, as a puppy, she used to chew on the drywall at their old home. Even when they brought her raw hides and other chew toys, the dog continued to chew on the walls. Finally, they figured she either was a very stubborn dog or needed more calcium in her diet. Milk gave her unpleasant side effects so, they resigned themselves to just patch the holes and, eventually, she grew out of that stage.

Josh brought her out of her thoughts. "OK. How are we going to get the logs here because, as you can see, there are trees up there." he said pointing at the hills behind the area. "Or we could drag them from below. It seems easier to let them roll downhill."

Envisioning themselves having to haul logs uphill, she said "Hum yes. We don't have domesticated horses, plus we would have to build something to carry them... it's too much trouble. Letting them roll downhill is best."

"Ok. We can use these to build the foundation." he offered, pointing to the boulders in the area.

Thinking through the problem, Sophie added: "We would still need to carry some the smaller stones from the lake for the floor and the fireplace."

"Do you know how to build a fireplace?" he asked.

"No idea... All I know is what I learned by watching a documentary about this little guy who went off into the Alaska wilderness and built a log cabin. We will just have to be very careful and take it one step at a time..." she said remembering the man and hoping that this place wouldn't get as cold, as it did there. Remembering the snow, she added: "We can also get gravel from the lake, to keep areas from getting muddy. It's not too far."

Josh frowned thinking about carrying the gravel. "We will need something to carry the gravel."

"Yeah... you are still talking about a lot of back and forth trips. We could use the tarp as a bundle." munching on a strawberry, she said then, she added: "We need carbs Josh.

These berries, beans and eggs will hold us for a while but, once we get started doing all that work, we are going to need more. I wish I could find some tubers, like potatoes..."

Josh felt that, somehow, that would not be a problem. "I think we will be OK Mom. I feel very good. Better than I ever felt before. I mean, we practically slept on the ground last night and I feel fine."

Sophie looked at her son. He had never slept on almost bare ground before. "You know you're right. Before, I would not have been able to move, after sleeping on the ground like that. I feel good too..."

Switching back to the subject of building the house, she said: "If we move the camp up here, we will save a trip. We can get water from the lake. I think we can catch a couple of those birds to bring up here. We can make a cage with twigs and ropes. With all that work, soon we will need to wash these clothes...?"

Josh shook his head. "Mom... I prefer to have a house first, then worry about clean clothes later. I mean, there is so much to do to prepare for the winter. So... we begin with one big room, right?"

"Yep. One big room with a fireplace. Tall enough for you to have head room." she joked, then she was lost in thought. "You are right." she said, finally. "We do have quite a bit to do before the winter. We have to gather food to store for the winter. We have to preserve that food... We will need wood for everything. That should be the first thing."

Josh stood up and stretched. "It's noon now. Sun's above."

Nodding, she sprang to her feet. "Let's go back down. I want to put some beans on the fire and start figuring out how we are going to get the trunks and the rest of the stuff, up here."

They had not given five steps, when Sophie stopped and began to look around. Lost in thought, she began to say, "We should also consider building an ice house, later on... Ice houses were used to store winter ice for use during the summer months..." The lake reminded her of their backyard pond and how it had frozen solid during winter.

Josh payed attention. He had learned that there was usually a good reason for her ramblings. He watched her move toward the back of the shelf. There, the shelf ended abruptly and portions of a wall of rock could be seen.

"You know... they actually used caves to store ice..." she said, taking a closer look at the rocks. "Josh, help me clear these vines aside."

Most of the rock had been covered by years of growth. Guided by something stronger than instinct, they worked with determination through the tangle. Little by little, they cleared away new growth, then old growth and, finally, there it was; the concealed mouth of a cave.

"Aha..." he said.

The cave entrance opened into a dry chamber with several rooms to either side. It was impossible to see anything beyond a few yards, so they decided they would have to come back with torches.

"It was so difficult to get in that I don't believe anything bigger than the dogs lives here..." she hoped.

They covered the entrance with branches, "Just so we can tell if any critters have been around here tonight." she said.

On the way back, Sophie picked thin branches for the chicken cages. She figured they could carry two birds in a cage up to the site. There were plenty of willow trees and cherry bushes, which provided strong pliable wood. Later, they could also lay branches in a zigzag, to use as fences to keep the birds to an area. It would be nice if they could get a couple of the goats to follow them up to the site. Goat milk would be a good supplement to their diet. Goats were also good to clear away vegetation; they were mother nature's lawnmowers and bushwhackers in one economical and environmentally friendly package.

4

GENTLE GIANTS

Back at the camp, the first thing she did was set the pot with water to boil. Then, she threw in two handfuls of beans. *Rice and Beans with water, again, tonight. At least today, we will, also, have fruit.* It had been a busy morning. She missed the conveniences of her previous life, specially showers. As soon as there was the chance, she was going to begin work on a bathroom.

Every time she thought of something they needed or would like to have, it was like opening a Pandora's box. Nothing was as simple as it seemed at first. To have a bath room, for example, would involve construction. She had a pretty good idea of how to bring up the walls of a log cabin. It was the roof what worried her.

The closest experience she had with roofs was putting together her backyard shed. *It can't even be called building because the thing came in pieces, packaged into a huge box.* All parts had been pre-measured and pre-cut to fit together. *Just follow the instructions, put the pieces together and you had a shed.* It had been harder to build the foundation for it.

Then there was the issue of water. How would she get the water from the lake? The prospect of carrying bucket after bucket of water was cumbersome at best. They didn't even have buckets. They would have to cut wood into shapes and try to figure out how to keep them together. She wished there were gourds to use as pails and bowls.

Waste would be an issue. They would have to dig a septic system. She did know how to make one, because she had followed the construction of the septic system at her grandmother's house, closely. Getting the water to the bathroom and the waste away from it was the real problem. She had no idea how she could design a working pipe system. What would she use for the pipes? She wished that whom ever dropped them here, would appear and help them.

There is such a thing as too much thinking. She had read somewhere that over analyzing situations kept the person stuck in a loop. The more the people thought about a problematic situation, the more issues they discovered which brought more questions; more "Hows" and "Whys"

"You're thinking too much." Josh had been watching her frown.

She turned and found her son and the dogs looking at her. How long had she been thinking? "You're right!" she said, springing to her feet and moving to grab a stick. "Let's get these cages ready."

Sometimes, the only way to stop the mind is to do something physical. Before the change, she would have taken the dogs for a walk. Thoughts generate chemicals, like adrenaline, and the fastest way to metabolize them is to burn them off through activity. Working together, it did not take them long to build two, simple but sturdy, cages.

Josh looked at the cages satisfied. "At least we have the cages now. If the opportunity arises, we can catch a bird and put it here."

"It will be about an hour before the beans are done." Then she saw the dogs. "Why don't you guys go hunt something?" The animals turned and bolted towards the river. Sophie stood quiet, watching then run. "What did just happen?"

"You told them to... go hunt... " Josh grinned, also watching the dogs.

Both looked on as the animals sniffed their way around bushes and tall grass.

"Do you figure they'll catch something?" Sophie asked.

"Hum yeah..." he said, remembering the rabbit.

She sat another pail of water on the fire then said: "I'm not sure but, if they do catch something, I'll fix it different this time."

Joshua's thoughts came back to the move. "We could also try to see if we can get closer to any of those goats and horses." he offered.

Sophie looked at the animals, eating calmly by the river. "That may be tricky..." Her eyes caught the dogs on their way back.

"Oh. No way... What is that?" She could hardly believe her eyes. The dogs bounced up and down in the grass with what looked like a turkey. When they surrendered their catch, Sophie inspected the bird. "This doesn't look like any bird I have seen before..."

Josh also found the animal different but similar. "Well, I know it's not a vulture; look at the beak."

Finally, Sophie sighed and said: "Aw' right. If this is the catch; this is what I'll cook." This time, instead of boiling the meat, she cleaned the bird, then she ran sections of it through, with a stick, and put it over the fire.

Josh indicated that, after the meal, he wished to go back to the clearing. He wanted to explore the cave further. They could use strips of tarp, tied around sticks, for torches.

"OK. Maybe we can also take one of the trunks with us." Sophie said, thinking that they could begin the move at the same time.

Josh considered the idea for a minute, then asked: "Which one?"

"The one that's nearly empty. We can leave it up there and use it to store items as we go." Sophie said.

Josh nodded. "Makes sense. Carry an empty trunk, then little by little bring the rest of the stuff?"

"I think it would be easier than trying to domesticate a horse." Sophie answered. Just then, Joshua's face lost expression.

"What is it?" she whispered fiercely.

Barely moving, he made a circular motion with his index finger. "Slow... turn slowly."

She did as told and came face to face with a huge dark eye. The gaze held for a moment of infinity. Finally, as if tired of waiting, the beast pushed his muzzle into her hands, giving her inexpressible joy. Gently, as if not sure if it was real, she raised her hand to the beast's huge mandible. She had seen photographs of Belgian Blacks but never one up close. This horse looked a lot like one of those.

"I wish I had apples for you..." she said softly. "If you come with us, we plan to live in a place where you would have access to an orchard... that's a lot of apples..."

"Goodness..." Josh exclaimed softly when another giant came to him.

Smiling at Joshua's reaction, Sophie said: "I believe these guys wish to come live with us, Josh."

"That's... so... amazing..." The boy's face was transfixed as he carefully ran his hand over the giant's rippling neck muscles. He had never been this close to a horse before.

Breaking off the spell, he quipped. "Do you think the chickens will be as easy?"

Sophie shook her head. "Well... that depends. What will you offer them, other than eating their eggs and maybe having one of them for dinner, once in a while."

Josh grinned. "So, how about we promise them we will never eat any of them."

"We shouldn't promise that, Josh. Birds reproduce like crazy." Sophie said, smiling.

"How about we don't eat the founding chickens." he countered.

"Ha, ha... OK, we'll see if you can sell them that deal, Sir." she said grinning.

Bear and the Termite were *less than impressed* with the horses. The Termite practically crawled to get behind her mistress; her wide eyes fixed on the beasts. Bear stood uncertain at a distance.

"It's OK boy..." Josh called to his buddy. Bear anxiously wagged his tail and came to stand on the other side of his master.

The horses ignored the dogs and calmly went to eat the grass, several yards behind the tepee. By the time they had finished eating, cleaning the utensils and around the camp, it was clear that they only had a couple of daylight hours left. If they went up to the mountains now, they would have to come back in the dark. Sophie did not feel confident about finding their way back and decided that it was best to have an early start.

"So we pack everything and move tomorrow morning then?" Josh said.

Sophie nodded. She thought about all they had to carry. "I'm not sure how we are going to get those trunks up there Josh."

Josh shrugged it off. He already had the answer. "We could tie them over the horses backs."

Sophie looked at the horses. They were big but the trunks were heavy. "You mean use the blankets as padding, tie ropes around the trunks and loop them over their backs? Wouldn't that be too heavy?"

Josh raised an eyebrow and gave her the one-eye look. "Mom, those are like draft horses. If they can carry me then, they can certainly carry the trunks."

"OK. I just don't want them to get hurt." she finally said.

Josh sighed at his Mom. *She would baby snakes, if she wasn't afraid of their poison.*

She took a pail of warm water and went inside the tepee. Her army days had taught her how to keep clean under less than optimal circumstances. Once refreshed, she disposed of the dirty water and set another pail for her son.

There was no polite way to approach the subject, so Sophie just blurted: "Josh, if you haven't done so, you really should wash your crevices with warm water. Bacteria collects in between the folds of skin and..."

"Yep. I got it Mom... Thanks." He gave her a thin smile and an exaggerated nod, before she went over the list of skin diseases, and the associated symptoms.

It is true that an image is worth a thousand words. He had experienced that principle, as a child. One day, rummaging in her office, he had discovered one of her medical books. Through the pictures, he learned, more than what anyone would ever want to learn, about skin and sexually transmitted diseases.

Fed, refreshed and with chores around the camp finished, they had little choice but to sit and watch the sunset. They both felt the urge to get up and go up the mountains, however, their rational mind told them that it would not be the wise thing to do, at this time. In silent contemplation, they sat until yawns overcame them.

She was back in the room with the stars above now. beside her, was the familiar presence of the man with the green eyes. There were other people with them now and they all stood waiting.

"Waiting for..." she began to say when her thoughts were interrupted by another.

"We are here to learn." the man with the green eyes said or thought. His lips had not moved.

The man gently held her elbow and, in step with the crowd, guided her to another room. There were rows of steep steps, where they found a place to sit. She looked at the man and he motioned for her to look to the front. There was the earth now and she realized that they were looking at a huge three dimensional projection.

The projection zoomed past the atmosphere and into a land where black men and women were being executed by black soldiers. Children laughed and splashed in the blood of the dead and the soldiers rewarded them with candy and guns. Mothers walked for miles, carrying dead babies. Their bodies, emaciated. There were trees and rivers, then the land became sparse. She saw people waiting in line in front of a huge silo. They held their bowls out for grain but only rats came out. There were places with palm trees, where people huddled together under the snow.

There were lands were people sat in front of huge tables full of food but the food was full of tiny worms. The people loved the food; they could not get enough of it. The worms traveled up their bowels and into their brains. The worms made them sick but the people didn't know it because the worms had taken their understanding away. They could only see certain colors and hear certain sounds and they were blind and deaf to everything else.

There were people who did not eat the food but still got sick. They cried and cried and couldn't go to work. They could not sleep at night and could not stay awake during the day. They had headaches, sore throats, chest pains, lower back pains and nausea. They covered their ears because they heard constant ringing. They covered their eyes because of the things they saw. She saw these people's skin loose color and become translucent like the skin that peels off a snake but instead, a whole person peeled off them. Once the other person had peeled off them, they were happy. They could eat the food just like everybody else.

The peeled off people were carried by the wind and floated above. She turned to her companion in horror. "Is that what we are?"

5

THE SHELF

She sat up and heard herself say with exasperation: "This is ridiculous..." It was dark still. The boy slept so it was probably very early. She got up and went outside the tent with the dogs following behind. The moon was low in the sky, so she figured the sun would not be too far behind. The large log in the pit had been reduced to mostly embers, so she decided to feed the fire. The dogs scampered off to check around the area.

How long would she have these nightmares? She knew that dreams were a way for the subconscious to bring up issues that needed to be examined but these, in a bizarre way, felt real. What had happened to them while they were away? She dropped the lemon grass into the pot of boiling water and stirred. The man with the green eyes felt real; all the other images had to be symbolic. *There's no way...*

"Mom?" Josh called from inside the tent.

"I'm here sweetie; just having some lemon tea." She turned to see her son peeking out of the tent.

"It's early." he frowned.

"Yeah, I know. Sorry. I just woke up and couldn't go back to sleep. The sun should be coming up soon." The sky was beginning to turn purple with nearing daylight.

"Oh well, I might as well get up then." He got out of the tent and stretched. "I'll be back Mom. Let me see if I can get some more eggs."

She gave him a winning smile. "I was hoping you would say that."

She thought of packing the tarps but decided to sit by the fire a little longer. She wanted to try to remember more about her dream. The man had said to look again, so she turned and saw how the peels had become real people. It had been the ones who remained, that became the empty shells.

The man had put his arms around her. It felt right to be in his arms. Everything about his touch and presence felt familiar, yet she couldn't remember ever meeting him. She had wanted to lean and stay in that embrace forever. The boy and the dogs approached, so she got up and went inside the tepee to get the frying pan.

Josh handed her the bowl with eggs, before sitting by the fire. "Here you have Mom. We have enough for today and tomorrow."

"Pretty good... we can put the extra eggs in one of the pails and pad around them with some straw, so they don't break during the move." They cooked and ate quickly because the sun was beginning to insinuate itself in earnest now. They wanted to be moved before noon.

It was easy to break down the tepee and pack their belongings. Joshua's idea of looping the trunks with ropes over the horses' backs worked just fine. He did get to catch a couple of the hens and they tied one cage on top of each horse. They left the poles stacked near the fire pits, drenched out the fires and began their move up the mountains.

It took them a little longer to reach the clearing, than the day before. Since the horses carried the weight, they allowed them to set the pace. Still, they were immensely grateful for their help. It was an experience to walk beside one of these giants. Incredible strong but gentle, they moved at a steady and leisurely pace.

Once at the clearing, Josh watched as the horses, now relieved off their cargo, ambled towards the lake. "They must be thirsty." he nodded.

Sophie wondered if the beasts would come back. She would have loved to ride one of them. Nevertheless, they needed to get their attention to more important matters. "Yeah... Let's get a fire started, then we can go and take a good look at that cave. Ok, Prometheus, where is that bowl with embers?"

They had brought embers to help them start a fire faster. Josh collected stones for the circle, while Sophie collected sticks. A couple of minutes later, they had a small fire going.

"That'll do for now. Let's go check that entrance." Sophie said, anxious to see if the branches had been disturbed.

The branches and dead vines where just as they had left them. *Good*, she thought. They cleared as much vegetation as they could reach above and about three feet to either side of the entrance. As they continued to work, it soon became clear, that the whole wall was a huge sedimentary rock formation.

Looking at the stones, Sophie tried to recall what she knew about type and placements of stones. "I have seen rocks like these before, but usually in arid places. If this is sandstone, then we may be in luck, Josh."

"How come?" Josh asked.

"Well, sandstone is more durable than limestone, so it would be a better building material." Sophie answered. She continued to study the stones as she worked. Sandstone would have been usually found in places that had been a beach or a desert. How had this type of stone ended in a temperate, maybe even cold, climate zone? *Perhaps there is an ocean not too far?* "Let's get torches, Josh." It was time to explore inside.

It took a couple of minutes for their eyes to become adjusted to the light of the torches. Once they were able to see clearly, they found themselves pleasantly surprised. Graceful curves of tan, red and browns extended before them.

Nodding appreciatively, Sophie said: "This is amazing, Josh. I have not seen colors like this since... what used to be Arizona."

Josh followed the patterns up and down the walls of the cave. "This is beautiful Mom...." Holding his torch high, he was able to get a glimpse of the ceiling. "How can that happen? It looks like a frozen chocolate, caramel and vanilla wave." he said, pointing to the swirls.

"Well... sandstone, like the name says, was mostly sand that became compacted. Continental drift continued... Layers of vegetation and dirt became compressed above the previous layers and that's how we have these beautiful colors... There was subduction, convergence, divergence... I guess we could call it a captured dirt wave."

To the left and right of the main hall, there were rooms like colorful, striped bubbles. Stopping by one of the rooms, Sophie said: "These are going to come handy for storage, Josh."

Further down, the hall curved to the left. They descended with care because, every few steps, the walls protruded at about shoulder height. After what felt like a long walk, they saw light and heard the rush of water.

"Josh, I think we are coming behind one of the waterfalls." Sophie said. Soon after she spoke, they saw the curtain of water. They were on a shelf that protruded under a waterfall.

Josh surveyed the area and said: "Mom, I think you have your shower room. We can set up this place to collect water for everything and also wash ourselves here. This works!"

Other than the passageway behind, she could not see another way to reach the area. She felt somewhat reassured that no one would drop by uninvited. The place reminded her of those expensive, naturalistic rough stone bathrooms. It was private and amazing.

"It sure does..." she said, assenting in appreciation.

He put his arm around her. "See... you think too much. We are going to be Ok." Then he gave her a little shoulder shake.

They were lucky. This cave was positioned just right to allow them to work on the clearing. They brought in their belongings and set small circle pits in the main room and another, in the shower room. Josh went off to gather more fruit, while Sophie set pots on the fire. She also collected stones with depressions in the middle, to use as oil torches. Outside, they cleared vegetation, with which they began a compost pile. The cave would do for now but they still needed to build a home. Josh didn't want to live in a cave for the rest of his days like some sort of primitive man. *Besides, soon, it will be too small to house the other... survivors?*

After lunch, they grabbed the axes and went to the hill above. There were tall pines, just thick enough to make for good building logs. Between chopping down the trees, cleaning them off branches and kicking them downhill, the hours went by. For a boy who had spent most of his idle hours in game servers, Josh surprised himself by how quickly he took to logging. It was grueling work but there was something in being able to test his strength that was deeply satisfying.

Watching him work this hard, reminded Sophie of when she was his age and felt indestructible *The first day of a workout, feels fantastic; it is the following days that can become a heartbreak.* She looked around and was glad to find birch trees. She had read somewhere that birch tree bark contained salicylates, a component of aspirin. She cut a section of bark and, feeling very survivalist, stored it in her pouch. *We can chew on a bit of this bark to help alleviate muscle soreness, if we need to.*

They stopped at 20 logs. Josh would have continued but Sophie motioned for him to stop. "That is amazing, considering that we started after lunch, Josh." she said.

Josh grinned. "It felt good Mom."

Sophie nodded, thinking that *there is nothing like an adrenaline high.* "Let's go back down. It'll soon be dark. Maybe we can move a couple of stones for the foundation."

Below, there were more than enough large stones to prepare a foundation for a log cabin. They selected stones of similar size and, together, rolled them to the right place. Then, they went to one of the logs and rolled it closer to the site of the cabin. They had selected an area, closest to the path coming from the lake, to the left of the cave. They placed the log over the stones and with a pail of water on top of the log, Sophie checked that the foundation stones were level.

"Ok, Josh. I think we need to call it a night." Sophie announced. They were tired but proud. It was amazing how much they had been able to accomplish in one day. If they continued at this pace, they might finish the cabin in less than a week.

It did not surprise her anymore when the dogs brought birds to her. She just cleaned and cooked them. She did notice that the dogs seemed to know better than to disturb the chickens. Sophie and Josh had built a pen for the chickens, which Josh named the "emergency chicken coop." Regardless, the chickens appeared content to stay in the area. At some point, Sophie went from noticing the unusual to expecting it.

After a light dinner of fruit, roasted bird and lemon grass tea, they gathered pine needles as cushion for the tarps they used as bedding. Later, they took turns in the shower room. Sophie absolutely loved to stand under the falling water and let all the dirt and shock from the past couple of days wash off her. The diluted soap-berry soap worked well on her skin and clothes.

Josh had taken a shower first. Play acting that he was a Roman Emperor, he had stepped into the main hall. "That was most refreshing..." He said with affectation.

"Since when did Roman Emperors have an English accent?" She had grinned, on her way to take her turn.

"Well... since... just now!" He had called after her.

After the shower, Sophie came back and found her spot. They had piled thick mounds of pine needles and placed the canvas tarps over them.

"This should be much more comfortable than back at the meadow, Mom." Josh said. Maybe you can get a good night's rest tonight?"

"Yeah, it would be nice..." Then realizing that she had not complained of not being able to sleep, she asked, "What makes you say that?"

Josh smiled. He loved being able to shock his Mom sometimes. "You have been having weird dreams, right?"

Sophie regarded her son with curiosity and said: "yes..."

Josh did a counting motion with his fingers and said: "First, you talk in your sleep; second, so have I."

Joshua's dreams had not been like hers. There were people, dressed like them, who rode horses. Instead of trunks, these people had been given duffel bags. A few stopped riding, then a different type of people came and hurt them. That's how he knew that they had to build. There were many others but some were not good.

Sophie wasn't sure that she had heard well, so she asked: "What do mean hurt them?"

Josh nodded and explained: "They attacked the people who dressed like us. They took their things and horses...."

"Then...?" she encouraged him to continue.

"They killed them Mom." Josh finally said.

That was not what she had expected. They had taken the poles near the forest, without thinking. The poles might have belonged to someone else! Sophie felt that she had allowed herself into a false sense of security. Even as she had advised her son not to wait for whomever had placed them here to appear, she had committed the same mistake. *How could I have been so careless?*

A thought came to her. "How could you tell them apart?"

"The ones who have been here for a long time wear animal skins. They wear necklaces and earrings made of fangs. They look like us but primitive. Their eyes are different. I can't explain; it's like they're angry. Oh, and they paint their faces. Our people just look normal, I mean, some have tattoos on their arms but no paint on their faces. The ones who have been here for a long time, do not have tattoos, instead, some of them have decorative scars."

Sophie frowned. "Decorative scars?"

Josh recalled the vision and nodded. "Yes, it's like they cut lines and shapes on their skin instead of using ink."

Lost in her thoughts, Sophie only muttered: "Hum."

"Can you talk about your dreams, Mom?" Josh had seen her toss at night and was curious.

She glanced quickly. She didn't want to worry him so, she said: "Well, I haven't had any dreams about this world. My dreams are about a place that I can't describe because I can't see it clearly. There is also a lot of people in my dreams. We all watch something like a three 'D' movie about the earth. I think my dreams are symbolic because the images do not make sense to me; at least not yet."

They stared at the fire in silence. Each considered what they had heard and it's implications. Later, Sophie laid on the canvas and said a silent prayer. *Please protect us and please give us a break. I'd like us to have a good night's rest.*

6

A HAPPY ACCIDENT

Perhaps because she asked for it or perhaps because she had been so tired, Sophie got her dreamless night. Maybe all she had needed was a good mattress. The pine needles bed had felt better than her old foam bed. She stretched carefully with no part of her body reporting pain.

Hum, she thought, *Another thing that's better about this place. Back on old earth, I would have been positively squeaky, after a day like yesterday.*

"Good morning!" Josh had changed into his clothes. "The clothes are dry, Mom. You go change and I'll get started on the eggs."

"Well, you're bright eyed and bushy-tailed today. Did you sleep good?"

"Yep. Love that pine needles bed." he said.

Sophie took care of her morning routine and changed into her clothes. Later, she would look into ways to get fibers to make more clothes, otherwise they would end up wearing skins, like the locals. That meant that they would have to hunt and she hated that thought.

Josh had become an expert at cooking camp fire scrambled eggs. "We have a full day of nothing but working on timbers, Mom."

She nodded and sighed. "I know... we need to cut down, at least, twenty more. I should be able to leave food simmering on the fire, so that all we have to do is get portions for lunch and dinner."

"Sounds good." he said.

They worked methodically. Knock down a tree, clean off the branches, roll downhill and repeat until the pile below needed adjusting. Once done chopping, they moved their operation down below, to the clearing, where they stripped off the bark and cut sections at the ends. Once a log was ready to be placed, they moved it closer to the site of the cabin.

The cabin began to take shape. They set a timber aside, over stones, and hammered a wedge in, to begin to split it from one end. It would take a couple of days to separate the boards, then another to smooth out major splinters, before they could use them to build the door and door frame. Instead of cutting through the logs, to leave holes for the door and fireplace, they created the holes on the go. They cut shorter sections of log and placed them crosswise, just like in the corners, to support the sections of wall around the door and fireplace openings.

Everybody had something to do. While the humans worked on building the cabin, the dogs went to hunt. Sophie and her son, took a break to prepare the birds.

"The dogs look like they're enjoying this new life a lot, Josh." Sophie said, looking at the contented animals.

Josh smiled at his buddies. They were good dogs. "It probably feels more natural for them, Mom. Plus you know they always loved to be outside with us, remember?"

"Yeah... You know we are blessed to have them, right? They are the guardians and the official hunters in the pack now." she said, petting the Termite. The dog, raised on her hind quarters, gently put her front paws on her mistress and looked up at her adoringly. "It never ceases to amaze me how loving these animals are..." Sophie said, looking into the Blue Heeler's amber eyes.

Grinning at the big lab, Josh said: "This guy is still a big baby with us." As if on queue, Bear came, meekly wagging his tail, to get attention from his master.

They worked until the sun above became too hot. Back in the shade, they shared a meal with the dogs and rested for a while. It was cool in the cave. Fearing that she would fall asleep, Sophie collected twigs for wattling, brought them inside the cave and worked on creating a grid.

Leaning on one elbow, Josh had been watching his Mom. "What are you doing Mom?"

"Well… since I have never built a fireplace I don't want to waste time with stones, just yet. However, I do remember how to make a mud house. I figure we can make the enclosure for the fireplace out of wattling and test it. That way, we can learn what it takes to make a good smoke stack." Sophie explained.

Josh imagined the result then frowned. "So, once we have a good design, are we going to leave it like that or cover it with stones?"

She nodded. Mud wattling needs a lot of maintenance. "Yes, I figure we will have to build a wall around it, with stones, to protect it. Wattling is basically dry mud and a good rain storm could damage the fireplace."

Josh continued pondering the problem. "But, what are we going to use to hold the stones in place?"

"Good question. First, we will look for stones with squarish shapes, so they can rest easier on top of each other. We could chisel them a bit. Next, we will look for clay to mix with ash and use as mortar. Clay is a type of mud that feels greasy when you rub it in between your fingers. It dries hard, like what you used in art class." Sophie loved these opportunities to teach.

"So, it is not just any type of mud?" Josh asked.

She smiled again. Her son was bright and curious and she had always loved these exchanges. "Correct. There is a type of mud that has more sand in it. I believe it was called muck. I am almost certain that clay would be better for the wattling."

"I see..." A shadow crossed over his eyes.

She noticed the change and asked: "What is it sweetie?" He looked at her and with a regretful smile said: "I was just thinking about all that you know. I know how you loved to read and how we don't have books anymore..."

Sophie waved an unconcerned hand. "Aw... sweetie... everything happens for a reason. At the time, I was just curious. Sometimes, I felt selfish wasting my time learning about things that I would never use and, guess what... I got plucked out of my old life and planted here. All that useless knowledge is getting put to good use now. See... civilized things, like books, happen precisely for the reason that you have just stated. People have kids, whom they love very much and want to help have a better life, so they try to teach them. However, one person cannot possibly know or remember everything so they figure out ways of preserving knowledge. I am not even sure that I remember things accurately. Practice will tell us."

"At first," She continued. "...people do what is needed to ensure survival. Later, when there is more people and chores are more evenly distributed, people find that they have time in their hands for exploration. That's what I hope happens here. When we have the basics covered, then we will have time to explore ways to make paper. We have an advantage because we already know what can be accomplished. We just have to figure out a way to re-create it."

Quietly Josh said: "I don't think we should try to re-create everything. I mean, there is a reason the old world is gone. There were many things that went wrong."

Sophie sighed. "Yes there were but right now we have a cabin to build. I'm not sure I want to remember the bad. It might take us too long... I don't know... it just feels like we should use our time to create. OK?"

With a thin smile he said: "Sure. I know what you mean. What good is it going to do us now, right?"

"Uhum." she nodded.

Sophie didn't tell him that she wanted to change the conversation because, in addition to feeling that it was not productive to rehash the negative, she wasn't sure about what had happened to the old world. The images in her dreams did not feel, entirely, like the past. What if there were more than one time line? What if the world continued, just without them? In addition, she didn't want to tell him that she felt that it would be almost impossible to have a perfect world.

If his dreams were visions, as she thought, then that would mean that, in this time line, there were humans who had very little regard for others. That meant that the seed for greed already existed. It would not be a stretch to say that, in a thousand years, this world would exhibit characteristics similar to those of ancient earth civilizations.

Many civilizations had started with lofty goals only to see them forgotten to greed and ignorance. *Perhaps books and the preservation of knowledge would be more than just a leisure activity?* Perhaps it was vital to preserve and communicate knowledge. But how could she control the dissemination of this knowledge, once she was gone?

Oh my freaking God... is that how this business of Torah, The Bible, Koran, Bhagavad Gita, Popol Vuh and all the books for the religious traditions got started?

Sophie felt thunderstruck. Similarities; parallels had been found in all of those books. The implications were so mind boggling, that she got up on her feet to shake off that train of thought.

She found Josh staring at the top logs in the cabin. "Trying to figure out how we are going to get more logs up there?"

Standing square with crossed arms, he said: "Yep. No offense Mom, but you're short."

"No, I'm not!" she said grinning. "You're just very tall. Back in the old world, I was actually taller than average for females. I had to be; boys get their height from their mothers, remember?"

Merely turning his head and pointedly looking down to her level, he said: "Yes, thank you mother. I still don't know how you're going to be able to help me lift a log up there."

She cut her eyes and asked: "Maybe if I climb on a small boulder?"

They managed to roll two boulders to the ends of the cabin and, carefully, use them as steps to lift the log into the highest rung. The technique worked well, until they got to the next level. In order to create head room, for anyone six feet and taller, they needed to stack ten logs. Almost on her tippy toes, Sophie momentarily lost balance. She saw, in horror, as Josh got pushed back by the log and was about to fall backwards. There were rocks behind him and, in a flash forward, she saw him hit his head against one. Something exploded inside of her and she yelled "No!" Next thing she knew, she was beside her son, cradling his head and his body, as he fell. "Humph!" She grunted. In a clatter, Sophie, Josh and the log hit the ground.

Almost immediately, he raised himself from over her and looked around. "Are you OK, Mom?"

Sophie sat up and noticed that the rocks, on top of which they should have landed, had been pushed to the sides. "I'm OK. Are you OK?"

Josh was amazed. "Yes. How did you get here so fast?"

"I... can't remember..." she said, uncertain.

Sophie got up and looked all around them, frantic to catch the beings who had just saved them. There was nothing, then she looked at the dogs. The Termite and Bear stood several paces away from them.

She stared at them for a moment. *Nah. They're too scared*, she thought. "I need to sit down." She felt lightheaded and nauseous.

Josh, trying to comprehend asked: "Mom, what just happened?"

She shook her head. "Josh. I don't know... I saw you hitting your head on those rocks..." She pointed towards the rocks that were too far now. "Those rocks were right here."

"I felt the log push me back, then I lost my balance and I heard you yell." Josh said, "Next thing I knew, you were holding me." He stared at her closer. "Mom, I had no idea what was going on. There is nobody else here. It had to be you. You did something..."

She felt the need for air. "Give me a minute, Josh. Could you please get me some water?"

"Sure." and he took off towards the cave.

Sophie stared at the fallen log, while she concentrated on her breathing. She closed her eyes and, in her mind, she saw the log. She found stillness. There was a strange pressure inside her head. It was not an unpleasant sensation; it was just an expansion. In her mind, she saw the log rise and settle in place at the top rung. The image was clear, vivid, as if her eyes were open. She felt a peculiar sensation in her whole body. It was like a rush of adrenaline. She felt good.

Sophie basked in the glow for a couple of moments, then slowly opened her eyes. Transfixed, Josh stood staring at her. The log was indeed in place. Sophie raised an index finger to her lips and motioned for him to join her. She took a sip of the water, he offered, before speaking.

"Josh... " Sophie explained to her son what she had done, then closed: "You said that I did something. I had to give it a try."

Josh leaned back, against the stack of logs, and whistled. "You mean to tell me that we could have done this all along, instead of all this work?"

Sophie exhaled in relief and let out a hearty laugh. She thanked the heavens above for her son. This boy was amazingly cool, under circumstances that would have sent any adult screaming.

"So... Master Yoda... when are you going to teach me how to do that?" Josh grinned.

Sophie laughed at the reference. Grinning, she quoted back: "Use the force Luke..."

They sat in good silence for a couple of minutes. After a while, Sophie began her interpretation of the Socratic method. In reality, she was helping herself state the problem. Sometimes the problem is not the obvious.

"Okey. How many logs have you cut down Josh?" she asked.

Josh frowned. "Hacking down a tree is not the same as lifting it in the air."

Raising one hand in gentle block she said: "Give me minute... do you have any blisters on your hands?"

"No." he answered.

"Yet, this is the first time, in your life, that you have swung that ax. You have worked for hours yet do not feel tired. What was going through your mind when you were swinging that ax?"

Going back in recall he said: "I was thinking about... nothing." Sophie continued. She asked questions as intuition guided her. "Did you envision yourself cutting down the trees, the night before?"

He nodded. "Yes."

"What did it feel like to swing that ax?" she asked.

Josh raised an eyebrow, surprised. "Actually, I thought I would hate cutting down the trees but it felt awesome."

Sophie continued trying to find an answer that would show her the block in his mind. "So, the night before you thought you would hate cutting down the trees but, when you actually did it, it felt great."

"Yes." growing impatient, "Mom...what are you getting at?"

"I'm not sure son... when I thought you were about to get hurt, something inside of me... went off. After that, everything's a blur. Do you believe that you can lift the log?" Josh quickly said yes, then realized that part of him did not believe that he could lift the log. Sophie nodded. There was part of the problem but she still did not know the cause of the block. "Why not?" she asked.

Grasping for words Josh related how he felt that his dreams might be visions. It worried him that people like them got killed. He had expected that whomever had taken them would still be around to protect them. If people like them got killed, then that meant that not everyone had the same abilities.

She agreed with him. "OK. I had an idea that something else was bothering you... By the way, I also feel that your dreams are visions. Normally, I would have been reluctant to admit that, because it sounds like crazy talk... but, I think that in this place, we left crazy behind a while back." she said, giving him a comical look of resignation, then she continued. "Listen... remember when we used to talk about how people of different backgrounds had different beliefs and how those beliefs affected their lives?"

He remembered. "aha."

"Josh, I am the same person that I was, before we got plucked."

After watching his Mom pluck chickens, he did not appreciate her use of the word. "Mom, would you stop saying that."

Sophie grinned. "Well, what else can I call it? We literally got lifted off the house and then... who knows. Anyhow... I have the same memories and pretty much the same beliefs that I had before... What is to say that our beliefs don't have something to do with how much, or even if, we can develop skills..."

Still the teenager, he countered. "Did you ever believe that you could lift a log with your mind?"

"Exactly Josh. Did you ever envision yourself hacking down over twenty pine trees in less than two days?" she answered.

He considered her last statement for a while then wondered aloud. "Why would anyone save people like us then bring them into an environment where they would not survive?" The whole thing was beginning to look like a cruel experiment, to him. "Why not teach them first, how to develop their own abilities?"

"OK. I think I can answer that. In my dreams, I find myself with a crowd staring at images in a screen. I also have the feeling that I have spent a long time interacting people. I think we all had something like a briefing... but, just like back in the old world, people heard what they wanted to hear. I am still myself in the dream. I still have the same thoughts, ideas and ways of responding to situations. I mean... I am still me. Does that make any sense?"

That didn't make sense. *Why would the aliens pick stupid people?* "Then why would they select people who wouldn't listen?" he frowned.

"Because... belief in the possibility of the impossible is not a pre-requisite for kindness." Sophie said simply.

Josh shook his head. "I'm not following."

Sophie didn't believe it was a matter of intelligence but of heart. "Maybe they just picked people who would try to help others." she said.

"So we are all good people who should be able to develop abilities but our beliefs can hold us back?" he asked.

Sophie nodded. There had been many intelligent people who had shown strong lack of ethics in the old world. "Exactly." she said. She hoped she was right.

They sat in silence for a while, until Sophie noticed that the dogs had left. *They probably went to hunt for dinner* she thought. "I think I want to try to lift another log. Do you mind?"

"Of course not, Mom. I'll watch from over there." he said, moving out of the way.

They had pre-notched enough logs that all Sophie was to do was concentrate and move them into place. She hadn't asked him if he wanted to try because she felt that he would discover his abilities, when the time for him was right.

Josh had watched her intently then, he said, "That was the last one. Next, we have to build the roof beams."

"I can't remember how the roof goes together, so I'm not sure that I want to tackle that now. Josh, how about we call it a day?"

So much had happened that day, that she felt drained. All she wanted to do was lay down and sleep but, of course, there was still much to do. They spent the rest of the afternoon gathering fruit and greens. Sophie also collected sticks.

"I want to practice building a little roof, before I try the big one." She explained.

Over the years, Sophie and her son had become a team of two. Each did their chores and then some. It came natural for them to look for ways to help the other. The result was that, even in this crazy place, they had soon created an evening routine.

Settled in for the night, Sophie and Josh worked on building the model of a roof. It turned out to be even tricker than they had expected. They had to adjust the pitch of the roof to work with the length of the logs, while making sure that it would be steep enough to discourage the accumulation of snow. Finally, they were able to put the mini logs together and create a decent model. They admired their little roof until they drifted off.

7

GREEN EYES

Sophie was back in the room with the sun and the stars. *Again?* she thought, then realized that now she was aware of the dream. She was the protagonist and observer. The scene changed and, with curious detachment, she saw herself laying on a bed asleep.

A man came into the room and watched her sleep. She saw how the man reached with one hand and caressed her face, then covered her mouth. Her perspective changed and now she was laying on the bed, looking up at the man. He had the same green eyes she remembered. She stared into those green eyes for what seemed like an eternity. *Why is he covering my mouth?*

In the distance, there was a noise and loud voices. *Please be quiet. I am not ready to wake up.* There was a flash and she fell back into her body. Green eyes had turned away from her to look at something above her head. Slowly, she stretched to look. There stood Josh, yelling something at the man. There was another flash and the man jumped away from her. All of a sudden, Sophie realized that this was not a dream. The commotion of yells and barks where too much and she yelled "Silence!" All sound stopped.

Josh came to her and grabbed her forearm. He said something but she could not hear him.

"I can't hear you but... I can hear myself." She realized aloud. Looking up she noticed that the man with the green eyes was in the cave with them. "Who are you?" She demanded.

The man took one hand to his throat and with the other, pointed at her.

She turned to her son and said: "Speak." Immediately she was able to hear him again.

Josh asked again: "Mom, are you OK?"

Sophie nodded to him. "Yes." Uncertain, she said, "Sound?"

Sound happened; the dogs barking, voices outside, even the crackling of the fire. The man with the green eyes turned to the voices outside and yelled something that made them stop. Turning back to them, green eyes said slowly. "Mein name ist Ulrich."

"Sind sie Deutscher?" She asked.

"Ja." He nodded, smiled then said something else, impossible to understand.

Immediately, she regretted using the few words in German that she knew. "I don't speak German; please slow down!" she said and raised a hand to hold back the flow of words.

"Obviously, you understand English so hold on one minute." Sophie turned to Josh and asked: "Josh, what happened?"

Tense, Josh narrated what he saw: "I don't know. I woke up and this guy was leaning over you. There was another man but I... "

Green eyes interrupted: "Your son tried to protect you. I apologize that we scared you."

They both turned and gave him a hard stare. "Why did you cover my mouth." Sophie asked.

"I didn't want you to scream." green answered.

Sophie frowned. The answer did not make him look any better. "Who else is out there?" she interrogated.

Just as fast, green eyes answered: "It is three of us. Can they come in?"

"No!" Josh and his Mom said in echo.

Ulrich raised both hands and nodded understanding, then he asked if he could sit and explain. Josh looked at his Mom, then turned and nodded to the man.

Ulrich explained that him and his group had found their first camp, then followed the stones. They found the cave because of the light of the fire. "I... dogs like me, that is why your animals did not alert you." he said.

Sophie looked around. The dogs were not around. There were no sounds of barking either.

As if reading her mind, green eyes said: "They are OK. They are outside with Iksha. She also is good with animals. I wanted to wake you up but I did not want to wake up your son. Not until I was sure that it was you."

Josh looked at his Mom, puzzled.

Sophie stared at the man then turned to her son and said: "I have seen him before..."

"Yes, you remember me?" The man looked hopeful.

Sophie's face remained impassive for a moment, then she said: "Please continue."

Ulrich had dark hair, was probably in his mid-forties and was a little taller than Josh. He related how him and his companions all had the same dreams. They dreamed about the room with the sun and stars. He also related part of the same dreams Sophie had but from his perspective.

"We come from different places. I am from Germany. We have Edgardo, from Spain and Iksha, from India. All remember a life before this one. We woke up and saw horses and bags. We all felt that we needed to travel... Later, we saw you two in a dream." he said.

"How long ago was this?" Josh asked the man.

Ulrich shook his head to one side and said: "Seven days ago."

They sat in silence, considering what they had just heard. "Roughly seven days away by horse..." Sophie finally said, "We do not have much time. We need to finish the cabin and begin building more."

"There is something you should know." Ulrich began. "Your son can manipulate fire; You can stop sound with your words. There is other people. They are people from this place and cannot do any of these things."

"Have you run into locals?" Josh looked up, alarmed.

Ulrich nodded to the boy. "Yes, and they are not friends. Iksha can look into that people's mind and know their thoughts. She said that the locals, as you say, have been here for a very long time."

Sophie, a little more awake, turned to Josh and asked: "You can manipulate fire?"

Ulrich grinned and regarded Josh appreciatively. "Your son threw balls of fire at us. I was able to protect myself but Edgardo could not." he said with a chuckle.

Joshua's face glowed. "Yeah, it happened very fast. I'm not even sure how I did it."

Turning to Sophie, Ulrich looked into her eyes, as if examining her. "How much do you remember me?" he asked.

Sophie stood the inquisitive eyes and stared back. "I remember sitting in a room looking at a huge screen with three dimensional images of earth. You sat by my side. That's it."

Ulrich looked at her for almost too long, then said, "I remember they said we would develop abilities. They said that everyone is different and that the skills would show at different times. They said, many times, to have good thoughts because we could create something we did not want."

"Who were they?" Josh wanted to know.

"I am not sure... There were several types of beings. I know a group was ascended beings. I can't tell you about the other beings." Ulrich looked almost as lost as they felt, when it came to knowing who were all the people in that room. "I remember many things but I have forgotten their faces."

Ulrich said that the invited had been kept in stasis for a while. Back on earth, volcanoes exploded; glaciers melted causing massive floods and tectonic plates suddenly shifted, causing world wide destruction. There was contamination from all the debris in the water.

The beings had to wait until the earth healed itself. The beings, went down to earth, periodically, to survey the progress. They said that there had been survivors to the catastrophe. The beings said that the survivors were corrupted. Later, they brought the invited out of stasis. Time moved slower in their world than on earth, so the humans would not age.

Sophie was about to ask him to explain what he meant by "corrupted" and if they told him why they had been spared, when, from just outside the entrance they heard a male voice.

"a'lo?" a deep voice with a thick Spanish accent called.

"Ja, Edgardo. I'm OK. We are talking." Ulrich called back.

The voice called back: "Can we come in?"

Ulrich turned to Josh and his Mom.

"Would you give us a minute?" Sophie asked politely, but firmly, as she motioned for the stranger to step outside.

Ulrich nodded and left so that Sophie could confer with her son. Sophie whistled the low call she had for her dogs and, soon after, Bear and the Termite came, wagging their tails, to sit by their masters. They looked relaxed and happy, as if enjoying the comings and goings around them.

Observing their behavior, Sophie said: "Josh, these guys were very good at telling friend from foe."

"I know... Well, what do you think?" he nodded.

Sophie shook her head. She did not like the way the stranger had chosen to come into their lives. "Either they are extremely good liars and they have even fooled these dogs or they are OK. I mean, we were preparing to receive others..."

Josh shook his head. He did not like it either. "Yeah. I'm just spooked because now I know that there are people we can't trust out there."

"Yes, that sort of puts a damper on the whole thing... OK, I'm calling them in. We won't get much sleep tonight, anyway... If anything... you can burn them and I can..." Lowering her voice, she added, "Let's not tell them everything that I can do, just yet. OK?"

"Uhum." Josh agreed.

"Hello?" Sophie called.

Ulrich poked his head in, "Ja?"

"Have your friends come in." Josh told him.

As tall as Ulrich was, so where his companions short. Josh and his mother, who had stood up to greet the newcomers smiled at the almost comical trio. Ulrich towered over a diminutive, but very beautiful, Indian woman and a stocky Spanish man with curly black hair.

Iksha didn't wait for introductions. "Sophia!" She yelled as she propelled herself forward with open arms. She hugged Sophie as if they had been a long time friends.

Edgardo was no less effusive. "Let me look at you muchacho." he said to Josh, appraisingly. "You are much taller than I thought!" Edgardo quipped, having to look up at Josh.

Josh and his mother did not know what to make of these expressions of affection. They did not remember these people, however, these people knew them... by name. Iksha and Edgardo were ebullient with happiness, while Ulrich smiled but held himself at a polite distance.

"We should prepare areas for you to rest." she said, reverting to the practical mode she sought, when she felt the need to create structure in a chaotic situation.

"Ah yes. We have to bring in the bags and things." Edgardo jumped in. "We will get your things, Iksha. You sit and chat with Sophia. Josh, come help us boy."

Sophie stepped forward. "No, we will all go." she said dryly.

Edgardo gave her a blank look, so Ulrich volunteered.

"Edgardo, Sophia and Josh did not have the same dreams we did. But they know about the marauders."

"Oh..." Understanding illuminated his eyes. "My apologies. You don't know if you can trust us... I understand, Sophia. A mother always protects her children." he nodded. Then he looked at Josh. "But you know this boy can defend himself, de verdad. I should know..." he said, as he touched the singed parts of his hair, alluding to his previous encounter with Josh.

Reminded of the fire ball incident, Sophie smiled but insisted. "That's OK. I could use some fresh air."

Outside, the air was as clear but a little less crisp. Satisfied that there were no others hiding, Sophie said to no one in particular, "Summer is around the corner."

As if on queue, Iksha added. "Yes, we have many seeds. We should begin planting tomorrow."

"Yes, we should." Smiling, Sophie replied.

Iksha and Edgardo had such buoyant energy that Sophia found herself having to adjust. While Joshua and Sophie loved humor, their personalities, in contrast, were much less exuberant. Sophie and Josh had spent a lot of time in their minds, so they valued introspection.

Over the years, Sophie had learned to allow Josh to set his own schedule. His school work had excelled, when he went to bed around seven and awoke at around three in the morning. He had loved the quiet early hours of the morning, when Sophie and the world slept. Sophie had, instead, chosen the hours while he was away at school as her personal time.

It had not always been that way. At one time, Sophie lived what people called "The Rat Race" She had worked hard and earned many awards and titles. She should have been happy, yet she felt miserable. The job, that she once loved, became like a prison. She became depressed. She began to suffer from migraines but the doctors could not find a cause. They prescribed medications, which caused side effects, for which she had to take, yet more medications. She began to feel as if her life had lost purpose.

In addition, people around her appeared to have gone mad. Many behaved in ways that could only be called evil. The way they lied and cheated, then rationalized their actions could not be explained as normal human nature. She also grew to dislike the way the news and entertainment appeared to focus on the tragic and dirty; the worst examples of human behavior. Looking back, later, she realized that it was her who had changed.

She took the plunge and left that world. It took her a couple of years but she was finally able to find her path; where she felt she was meant to be. Sophie learned to ignore advice that would keep her boxed in. After much research, she realized that she was not the only one who had felt that something had to change. There had been millions of people looking for meaning in their lives.

"Sophia...?" Iksha had come to stand by her.

Snapping back into the present, Sophie bent her head to look at the tiny Iksha. "Yes, what can I do for you?"

"These are my friends." Iksha smiled.

Sophie's eyebrows shot back. Standing by Iksha were four goats. "Your friends?" She was good with animals... Iksha had just asked the goats to come with them and they had followed.

"They are very good to have around, you know..." Iksha went on. "They give us milk and they eat everything. They will be able to clear vegetation for us to plant."

Iksha had just mirrored her previous thoughts. Sophie nodded appreciatively and said: "That is... wonderful."

Ulrich and Josh began to unload the horses. They had tied and looped the bags over the horses' backs, like Josh had done with the trunks. There were many bags. Josh untied several bags and handed them to Edgardo, who could not reach that high. Edgardo made up with enthusiasm, what he lacked in height. Quickly he took the bags inside the cave, then came back running for more.

"Vamos muchachos! I want to get some sleep!" he called to Ulrich and Josh, while beating his hands in a move-fast gesture.

Sophie handed a bag to Iksha, from the fourth horse and asked her, "What else do you have here?"

"Oh... you will love it Sophia. I have been collecting seeds, plants and stones on the way here. I even have a stone that we can use to give ourselves a pedicure."

"You mean pumice stone?" Sophie hoped.

"Yes, pumice. I also found nut trees and collected a lot of the fruit. We can eat some and plant some." Iksha said with a winning smile.

Smiling back at Iksha, Sophie began to feel the tension between her shoulders relax. During the past two days, She had raked her brains to remember everything she could about plants and their uses. With Iksha here, it sounded like she could step aside and allow her to take over the management of plants and gardening, if she so desired.

They placed the bags with extra supplies inside the first room to the right. Ulrich, Edgardo and Josh had finished carrying the rest of the bags inside the cave also. Once all five of them stood around the fire, Sophie indicated where they could find the shower room.

"They will need more wood for the fire. I'm willing to bet that, at this time of the night, that water is probably very cold." Josh stepped in.

"Uhum." Ulrich said and immediately moved to get more wood.

Edgardo began to prepare sleeping areas for himself and his companions, while Iksha unwrapped flat bread.

Sophie opened her mouth in a wide ooh... " You found wheat?"

"Yes!" Iksha said, smiling from ear to ear. "...and I have seeds!" she added.

"Oh, that is so wonderful!" Sophie plopped down on her bed with tremendous relief. "All we have is beans and more beans."

"Nothing wrong with that!" Edgardo turned, smiling.

Josh grinned, then turned to step outside. "I'm going to help Ulrich." he said. Josh found him standing near the edge of shelf, looking down into the lands below. "Hello..." Josh walked up to meet Ulrich.

"Hallo Josh." Ulrich greeted Josh.

"See anything?" Asked Josh nodding towards the lands below.

Ulrich had not been trying so much to see but to feel his surroundings. "No, nothing much." he said quietly. To himself, Ulrich thought, *animals... the horses by the lake... other animals. No humans other than us, yet.*

As if reading his mind, Josh asked, "Do you have any idea how long before we have more people coming to join us?"

Ulrich was vague: "I can't tell... a week...maybe."

"Hum." Josh nodded. They stood in silence for a minute, until he could wait no longer. "Ulrich, you mentioned another world..."

The man gave Josh a side glance. "Yes, there are worlds, other than earth."

"...and the people who... took us, are from another world." Josh finished.

"Yes, and no." Ulrich shook his head a little. "They live in a different world and a different time. It is time that happens at the same time as our time. It is not easy to explain."

Josh had an idea that Ulrich was talking about dimensions and, yes, that would be difficult for anyone to explain. "It's OK. Did they tell you that we could get killed?"

Ulrich nodded firmly. "Yes. They talked to us and told us about the marauders."

Marauder is a term for wanderer and thief. Josh wanted clarification. "The corrupted survivors?"

Ulrich nodded again. "Yes, they also said that this planet had been through a transformation and that there would be plants and animals like those we remembered but also different."

Josh wanted to know if his theory was sound. He asked: "Is this earth?"

Ulrich looked at Josh and said. "Again, yes and no..."

Josh nodded. Sophie had raised Josh away from the dogma of church but in touch with God. His Mom had read to him John 14, where it said: "In my Father's house are many mansions..." so the boy did not find conflict between belief in the divine and the possibility of other worlds.

After a pause, Ulrich continued. "They are not aliens, like little green men, Josh. They are us. They said that they didn't choose us. They said that we chose ourselves."

Josh groaned at that answer and Ulrich laughed with him. "I thought the same!"

Laughing at the impossibility of the situation, Josh and Ulrich finished collecting the wood. Josh asked him several more questions that Ulrich answered patiently. They carried two armloads of sticks into the cave and joined the group.

The newcomers enjoyed their first shower room experience. One by one, they had excused themselves and reappeared later with smiles and wet hair. It almost looked as if a toga party was about to take place in the cave. Their clothes, left hanging near the heat of the fire, would be dry by morning.

"I like what you have done there!" Iksha purred.

"I could help with some stone work." Edgardo volunteered.

"Oh..." Sophie looked at him, inquiringly.

"Yes, I was a stone carver back... before." He continued.

"And what did you do, Ulrich?" Sophie asked, addressing Ulrich for the first time, since they had gone to get the bags.

"I did many things..." he said vaguely, then added. "But I worked with wood."

Nodding, Sophie looked around the room. "It sounds like we have more than enough skills in this room to help us build a settlement."

"Well, that's good. I don't know about ya'll but I'm getting some sleep. Good night!" Josh said, almost deadpan.

"Yes, it has been a long day." Edgardo followed and also turned in.

Iksha, politely said good night and also laid down.

It was Sophie and Ulrich left. Ulrich sat with his back to the wall and stared at her. His face was serious but open. It was as if he was trying to read her mind. Sophie shifted, uncomfortable under that gaze. In her dreams, it had felt right to stand beside him and allow him to guide her, however, what she felt now was closer to apprehension.

Finally, she propped herself on her side and stared at the fire. Sophie stared at the fire until she no longer could. It cannot not be called sleep, what she fell into. Back in her Army days, she had been able to stand guard, in semi-consciousness, for hours. Tonight, her state was similar. She drifted into a world of images, then fought them back to return her attention to the cave. It was useless to try to remember the images; they went by too fast.

She checked that every one else was still in the same position. There was her son's soft snore; Edgardo's little lumber mill; Iksha's sighs and even Ulrich's deep respiration. Chagrined, she wished she could sleep.

8

THE GIFTS

Ulrich had started a fire outside, when he heard muffled tones coming from the cave. He collected his friends, before they woke up Sophia and Josh. Back at the fire, he said. "They have chickens..." he pointed towards the eggs he had collected earlier.

Turning to Iksha, Edgardo asked, "Iksha... don't you have coriander in your bags? We could make seasoned eggs... and with the panecitos, meat... a little tea..." He entreated to her.

"Yes, Edgardo... I"ll cook breakfast." Iksha feigned mock annoyance.

"Right. Is there anything else we can get for you, Iksha?" Ulrich cut in.

"No, thank you dear. What will you do now?" Iksha said, leaning back to get a good a look at his face. She actually had to hold on to his forearm, to keep her balance.

"I think I will take a look at that cabin." Ulrich nodded towards the unfinished log cabin. "We will need many more buildings. Edgardo, can you see where we can find more stones?"

Edgardo's countenance immediately became business like. "Yes, we do not touch this cave today. I'll take one of the horses and have a quick look around."

Each went to work and after about an hour, they met back again. Edgardo had inspected the area above and left of the cave. Iksha had busied herself making more bread.

"They will probably sleep until late this afternoon." Edgardo said, as he joined Ulrich and Iksha by the fire.

"It will be longer than that. I gave them some tea." Iksha said, looking in Ulrich's direction.

"She is not going to be happy about that, Iksha..." Ulrich sweetly frowned at her.

"Only if you tell her." Iksha retorted.

"Well, dear... What do we have?" Edgardo asked, sitting down beside her.

Iksha raised one eyebrow. "Have you washed your hands yet? Do you want to get sick? What do you mean what we have!" Iksha mock scolded him.

Smiling, Ulrich flashed high eyebrows to Edgardo and both went to wash their hands. From the moment they had awaken, in the middle of the woods, Iksha had made it clear that she would not be trifled with. They had grown to adore the diminutive dynamo.

Iksha had made sure that the men kept themselves clean and didn't take unnecessary risks. She always addressed Ulrich lovingly but feigned annoyance with Edgardo, who enjoyed their repartee immensely. It was clear that she found the Spanish man very attractive, however, she was not about to tell him. A woman could get hurt.

"There is another waterfall, above this one here..." Edgardo pointed in the general direction of the shower room. "...behind that..." he continued, in between bites. " there is another lake with huge rock formations. We could quarry rock from there. Transportation may be an issue."

"Sophia might be able to help us with that." Ulrich volunteered.

"Oh?" Iksha raised an eyebrow in questioning. "You haven't told us all you know about Sophia, dear."

"Yes... I wanted to wait." Ulrich looked a little troubled. "Sophia does not remember as much as I do."

"What do you mean?" Iksha gently prodded.

"Well... she doesn't remember... what she can do... me." Ulrich said.

"Can you, somehow, help her remember?" Edgardo gave him a knowing look.

Ulrich slowly shook his head. "We were told we shouldn't do that, remember? None of us should force another to remember."

Iksha gently squeezed his forearm. "It will be Ok dear. We are not going anywhere." Had Iksha read Ulrich's thoughts, she would have realized that she had voiced his concerns. Looking at the cabin, Ulrich said that they could finish it by themselves and let Sophie and Josh sleep.

"Iksha. Edgardo and myself can do this work, if you would like to go and collect your plants."

"Yes. I also have to put my goats to work." she nodded.

Later on the day, Josh woke up and found himself alone with his mother. "Mom... Mom." Josh gently shook her shoulder.

Sophie stirred and took a deep breath. "Wow... I needed that." She thought, then remembered the newcomers. She sat bolt upright. "Where.... How long have we slept?"

Outside, Ulrich stopped his work and looked up. "She's up." They had made good progress, perhaps it was time to take a break. "Edgardo, I'm going to check on Sophia."

"Very well, I will see if Iksha could use a little company." Edgardo said, with a wink.

Ulrich nodded. Those two had a way of making him smile. They had kept him entertained during the long ride here.

There is love between those two. He thought. So absorbed, was he in his thoughts, that he almost bumped into Sophie.

"Hallo..." He stopped short. *Why can't she remember me?* He felt her apprehension and confusion. It frustrated him that he could not help her remember. Each one has a path. It is counterproductive to tell anyone, unless they ask.

"Hi... sorry we overslept..." she said clumsily.

Josh came up from behind her. "That felt good. Thank you for letting us sleep; we needed that."

Ulrich grinned at Josh. He liked the boy. He was obviously very comfortable in his skin but was, at the same time, helpful and polite. "We have some food left, if you are hungry." Ulrich offered.

Josh returned an exaggerated nod. "Yes, I am... very."

Sophie realized that she was very thirsty. "I could use a little water." she said.

Ulrich walked them to the outside fire. On the way, Sophia noticed that the cabin was finished. All that was needed, were finishing touches. She took the bread and tea that Ulrich offered to her, then turned to take a closer look at the cabin. Ulrich left Josh, content with a wrap and tea and went to join her.

"How did you get the logs up there? Did Josh wake up, before I did, and help you?" Sophia could not believe that little Edgardo had been able to raise those logs.

"No. He slept as much as you did." Ulrich said, searching into her eyes.

"...but how..." She looked at him. It was disconcerting to look into those green eyes, for too long. She felt as if she was in two places at the same time. She was here, beside the cabin and she was in the room with the sun and the stars. Her mind was not ready to follow those iterations, so she turned her gaze to the roof of the cabin.

Ulrich began to explain, "We used two poles as ramps and..."

"Oh.. I'll be... why didn't I think of that." Sophie interrupted. Shaking her head, she turned to Josh. "Boy... I'm telling you... sometimes your mother..."

"Hum?" Josh frowned.

"Instead of almost killing us, I could have used two of the timbers, to roll up the top timber."

Ulrich, having finally understood the interaction, broke into a wide smile. "That is Ok. You didn't have experience." he said kindly.

Sophie sat on a boulder and stared into the distance. There was something about what Ulrich said that didn't sit well with her. She thought about it for a minute then commented. "That is not good... Does that mean that we will have to wait until people with the right skills and experience come to join us, before we can advance past a basic settlement? There are so many things that are needed..."

Sitting across from her, Ulrich leaned forward. He understood her concern. "No, we can use the power of intention to create things. I saw that you built a little roof..." he said. Sophie nodded so he continued: "That gave you the experience you needed to visualize the finished product."

Sophie turned to look at him. "Explain to me about the power of intention, please."

Ulrich nodded. "We all have skills, abilities..." He continued. "I know that you can do more than just stop sound."

Giving him a blank stare, she asked: "What makes you say that?" Sophie wondered if he could read her mind.

"Everything in the universe is a vibration. If you can manipulate one type, you can manipulate all the others..." he said, looking straight into her eyes. "Sound is a vibration and you can manipulate that already."

Trying to keep from letting her relief show, Sophie asked, "How?" Sophie wanted to learn to manipulate the vibration peacefully. Both of her previous experiences had been under stressful circumstances.

Ulrich's voice brought her back to the present: "You have to quiet your mind and focus on an idea, for example, if you wish for an apple, then you must remember the apple... The idea of an apple. Is it red or green? Does it crunch, when you bite into it? Is it juicy? Is it heavy in your hand or small? Imagine what it feels to have the apple. Appreciate having the apple..."

The world around them lost focus. There was nothing but green eyes and the apple. Sophie felt lighter and happy. She could feel and smell the apple in her hand, while at the same time, she felt drawn into those green eyes. She wanted to stay in that place forever but she couldn't. Blinking she became aware of her surroundings again. Josh, Iksha and Edgardo stood watching them in silence. Ulrich reached towards her, grabbed an apple from her hand and bit into it.

"Nice..." he said with a wink. The apple was so juicy that, a little embarrassed, he had to wipe a drip off his beard.

Iksha was besides herself with joy. "Oh Sophie! That was wonderful!"

Josh came to face his Mom. "...and we have been eating rice and beans?" he said with raised eyebrows.

"Aw... I didn't know!" Laughing, Sophie hugged her son.

"Sophie..." Edgardo asked gently. "How do you feel?"

Appreciating his concern, she nodded. She felt OK; there was no feeling of being drained. She then looked at Josh and began to relate the log incident.

"Yesterday..." Sophie began to say, then turned to Josh to make sure he agreed to share more information. Josh nodded encouragement. "Josh almost got hurt because I suggested that we step on rocks to reach the top rung." Josh gave her shoulder a gentle squeeze. "Anyway... I lost balance and pushed Josh..."

Sophie related the incident and how, later, she discovered that she could move objects, even if she was not under stress.

This time, it was Edgardo who turned to Ulrich and said. "And we didn't have to do all that work!"

"That's what I said!" Josh chimed in.

Ulrich stared at her for a minute, then inhaled deeply and said, "Let Iksha and Edgardo show you what they can do."

Following his queue, Iksha beamed, "Yes, let me show you my garden!"

"Garden?" Sophie raised both eyebrows and followed the tiny figure. At the far end of the shelf, right before the path to the orchard, there lay row after row of baby plants. "How..." Sophie began to ask, then she gave up. It seemed that everything was possible in this place. "You must love plants." she told Iksha.

"That's what Ulrich said. I have always loved to garden and learn about plants. Perhaps that is why I can do this." Iksha glowed with happiness. It was happiness and she actually glowed. At first, Sophie thought her eyes were fooling her, until Josh mentioned it.

"Iksha, you're glowing." he said.

"Thank you." she smiled to the boy.

"No, I mean you really are glowing, as in, something is radioactive and glows?" he said, looking worried now.

Ulrich couldn't help but laugh. "It's OK Josh. We can all see it. "

Josh frowned and turned to him. "...and how is that good?"

Laughing out loud now, Ulrich explained that all objects generate a glow but that he could not see it before. His abilities were developing and that meant that he would be able to see more than he could before.

"Did I ever mention anything about auras, Josh?" Sophie asked her son.

"No, or maybe I don't remember." Josh said, mesmerized by Iksha's glow.

"Look at something else, sweetie, but don't focus on it. Try looking at the edges of things." Sophie advised.

Joshua rested his eyes for a couple of seconds on her then Ulrich, Edgardo, the dogs, goats, plants and rocks. "I see glows of different colors." he finally announced.

"Ok, now brace yourself; it gets more interesting." Ulrich patted him on the shoulder. "Edgardo?"

With a little ceremony, Edgardo picked a rock and, before their eyes, molded it into a cylinder. "Would you say this could work as pipes to carry water, Sophia?"

"How did you know?" she asked, now worried that *he* might be able to read her mind.

"We saw you in a dream, sitting right here and talking to Josh about how to build a log house." he said.

"OK..." she sighed, then, "Wait, you saw me? So the dreams are visions. Can we consciously see each other in our dreams? Could we see who else is here?"

It was Ulrich's turn to answer, "Yes, Josh can do that."

They all turned to Josh. At first, he thought of deflecting their attention, then decided that it was not a good time for jokes. "I have not tried to see the others. I have dreams about them but it has not been intentional."

"It's OK. I will come to you." Ulrich told him then, with sudden urgency, he brought them back to the subject of building a house. "We need to talk about a bigger shelter; a house with several rooms. None of us has built a big house before. We should make a model first."

Becoming animated, Josh suggested, "What if I get pebbles from the pond and we try to build a castle? ...or maybe a large stone house?" He had always wanted to visit a real castle.

"Why not..." Edgardo agreed.

"Let's go then." Iksha also agreed.

Ulrich asked Sophia to stay back with him. The others turned and left them alone. When the others were out of earshot, Ulrich turned to Sophia. "Be kind to yourself, Sophia. Maybe that was the way for you to discover your abilities."

Sophia stood with her arms crossed. She looked at him but didn't say anything. She wondered why did he care how she felt.

Ulrich tried to reassure her. "You kept your son safe." Then, a shadow crossed over his eyes. "I have also made mistakes here."

Sophie noticed his troubled look but said evenly: "I will be as kind to myself, as you are to yourself."

He stared back at her. "You are right. It is not easy to let go of guilt."

Sophie realized that she had been harsh. "I am sorry. I know that you are trying to help me..."

Ulrich held out his arms. Surprised, Sophie realized that she could not have held back, even if she wanted. She stepped forward and accepted his embrace. They hugged for what felt like a very long time.

"Sometimes, words are not enough..." he said, as he rested his head on hers.

"There are no coincidences..." Sophie said, as if repeating a previous conversation.

"...and everything happens for a reason." finished Ulrich, still holding her.

She could have stayed there forever. It was, surprisingly, nice and safe there. She felt him stir and reluctantly stepped back. "We must get going. There is still much to do..."

His eyes had a glint now, but he merely said. "Yes, the others are waiting."

They met the others by the outside fire. "What do you say, Ulrich; outside or inside?" Edgardo wanted to know where to take the bowls of rocks and a bit of mud.

"Outside. I think it would be best. Let me make a platform." Ulrich said, moving towards the pile of leftover wood.

Iksha came to stand in between Sophia and Josh. "Watch this guys." she said, looping her arms around theirs.

Ulrich picked several scraps of wood and held them together. The ends grew fibers which reached and met each other. Little by little, a bigger piece of wood was formed. Ulrich, slowly ran his hand over it, in a sweeping motion. When he was done, the fibers in all the pieces, were lined in the same direction. It was impossible to tell where there had been a separation. He placed the platform, on top of a flat stone, close enough to use the light of the fire.

"Wow, that is beautiful…" Sophie ran her hands over the surface. "So, you love wood."

Ulrich smiled at her and his green eyes held her for a moment. "Yes." he finally said.

"Can you do that with any wood; even dead trees?" Josh asked. He had always loved trees and his preference was to avoid cutting them.

Turning to Josh, Ulrich said: "Yes. All wood is fibers. Dead trees have less moisture than standing trees. All I have to do is borrow moisture from the air."

"Thoughts and words become things." said Sophie, absently.

"Believe it and you will see it." Echoed Ulrich, staring at her.

A thin smile on his face, Josh glanced from his Mom to Ulrich.

9

THEY MOVED STONES

The next day, they all slept in. Building the Castle had turned out to be more complicated than any of them would have guessed, so they stayed awake, late into the night. There were so many considerations, beginning with the foundation and water systems. Sophia had insisted in having a basement for cold storage.

"We must have a place to keep food and stone basements are very cold." Sophia had insisted.

"We don't need storage, Sophia. Didn't you demonstrate that we can create our own food?" Edgardo had insisted.

"Edgardo, have you created food?" She asked.

"Hum. No." He admitted.

"Why do you think that is?" By now, Sophia had a theory about what was necessary for their abilities to develop. She knew that Edgardo loved food but never worried if others had eaten.

"I... don't know." He finally said. It was true, he had tried but failed miserably. The only ones that he had seen create food, had been Ulrich and Sophia.

"Ok then. What if I'm not here? What if something happens to me?" Sophia had insisted.

"Why must you worry so much, Sophia?" Edgardo exhorted.

"Edgardo, there is a method to my madness. I can't tell you right now why we need a basement because I'm not sure myself. I just know that it feels right to have one." She stood her ground.

Once they figured the design for the foundation and the basement, they moved on to the water systems. There had to be two separate main pipes, one for clean and one for dirty. The clean water pipes split into cold and hot. They would heat the water in a stone tub, because none of them could work metal. Sophia insisted that every design be made considering people without abilities. Edgardo was about to object, when Josh and his Mom said in chorus, "It just feels right!"

They spent hours considering every detail, then building the model. Edgardo made the little stone parts, while Ulrich, the little wood parts. Iksha reminded them of proportions. She advised on the size and location of the rooms, according to function. Sophie, moved and mortared the pieces into place. Josh helped them test the hot water system, by creating a tiny fire under the water tub. They all watched in fascination as steaming hot water came out of the tiny pipes.

"Hopefully, we won't allow the water to get nearly that hot..." Sophie thought aloud. Ulrich considered what she had said and agreed. "We need to make sure this place is safe for children."

Edgardo and Iksha quickly glanced at each other, then away. Sophie looked at her son and hoped that there was a good girl, and happiness in his future. She certainly would love to see grandchildren run around the place.

All the while, Josh had been lost in thought. The vision cleared and he said, "There are no children in the groups, yet. There are young couples and singles; there are mature couples, but no babies. I have seen kids, like tweens, but that's it."

"Did you do that on purpose?" Sophie asked her son.

Josh gave her a sheepish grin. "Kinda. I just wondered if there were children in the groups, then I stared at nothing. Next thing I knew, it felt like my head was expanding and images came to me."

Sophie nodded appreciatively to her son and said, "Nice." Then turning to the rest, she added " It is a good thing that we won't have babies to worry about, yet. Children will come later. Children always come."

Today, Josh was first to rise, followed by Ulrich and the dogs. They collected eggs for breakfast and Ulrich produced fruit and meats. Josh exercised his new found skill and started the fire. *I wonder what else can I do?* "Ulrich, how can I discover if I can do more things?"

Ulrich was glad to have a chance to chat with Josh. "Like in life, Josh, it is not a matter of if you *can* do more things but if you *want* to do more things. What I mean to say is that, back in the old world, people studied many things but only became very good at the ones they loved."

"Well, I was very good at math but I didn't love it at first. I learned to love it when I became good at it. I had to practice it. Is that also a way?" Josh challenged.

"Yes. There are many ways. We can learn because of a traumatic experience, like when you thought I would hurt your Mom... We can also learn by study and practice."

Josh ignored the opening and insisted, "If that is so, then how come Edgardo cannot make food?"

Ulrich saw that Josh was not ready to trust him. He decided to let Josh approach the subject of his own, when he was ready. He answered Joshua's question, instead: "Edgardo would want to make food for himself. He is a very kind man, but he does not worry about feeding others. Food is nourishment. Edgardo has not made the link between nourishment and love."

"So, there are limitations." Josh asked.

"Yes, if our intention is purely selfish, then we cannot make things happen this way." Ulrich liked Josh. Like his Mom, Josh had a very analytical mind. In spite of which, he did not share that there was a lot more to creating through intention. Ulrich felt that it would not be appropriate to discuss those areas with a young person.

One by one, the others joined them. They joked about the little castle and how much trouble it had given them. Then, the conversation turned to practical things, such as, where would they get the stones and the trees they needed.

"I know where to get the stones, and I can cut them but, I cannot carry them." Edgardo said.

Ulrich deadpanned, "Sophia and myself can lift the stones."

Edgardo raised both eyebrows. He turned to Ulrich and practically demanded: "How come you didn't tell us that yesterday?"

Ulrich waited a minute for their surprise to subside. "I can't tell you why... but I had to wait until Sophia discovered that she could..."

"What if she never discovered that she could?" Edgardo asked, assuming that Ulrich had meant to say: "to lift the stones."

"I hoped that she would." Ulrich said, looking at Sophia.

Annoyed, Edgardo shook his head. "OK. So, both you and Sophia can help us. That's good. What else?"

Iksha put a hand on Edgardo's forearm and turned to Ulrich. "What can we do to help dear?"

Ulrich turned to Sophia and said, "Sophia and myself will sit above, on the hill, so that we can have a view of this area. Edgardo will cut the stones and call our names, when the stones are ready to be lifted."

"Call your name? I can't yell that loud." Edgardo frowned.

"We will hear you, Edgardo." Ulrich reassured him. "Iksha, you should stay below so that we can get a view of the progress, through you. Josh, you should go with Edgardo.

You should be within eyesight of Edgardo, but out of the way from the stones. None should ever step under the stones, when they are in the air."

Edgardo, Josh and Iksha looked at them dumbfounded. What Ulrich proposed did not sound feasible. They would be miles from each other.

Josh looked at his mom. If she was Ok with it, he would also be Ok. "Mom?"

Sophia thought about all that Ulrich had said. She had an idea that Ulrich would be able to see and hear them at a distance. However. in spite of remembering how safe it felt to be in his arms, she was not entirely ready to trust him. Instead of openly challenging his idea, she asked a what-if question. "Ulrich, what happens if we are distracted?"

Ulrich nodded. "That's why we must be very careful. You and I will be able to see and hear them. While one is moving a stone, the other will keep an eye on the others." He didn't want to go into splitting focus yet. Sophia nodded. She understood better. She only hoped that she was up to the task.

They sat in silence, each thinking about what had just been discussed. Iksha, Edgardo and Josh felt anxious but excited about what was about to occur. Sophia had many questions to ask Ulrich, but she felt it would be better to wait. If she asked questions now, it might look as if she did not have faith in Ulrich's abilities. It would be counterproductive because she knew that the others needed to have faith in their abilities.

"The sun's getting higher" she said, "If we are going to do this, we should get going." She stood to indicate that she was ready.

Iksha reached for the pots, to clean them, until Ulrich motioned for her to stop. "Sophia! Visualize them cleaned." He instructed.

Sophia's head shot in his direction, then she met his gaze. His eyes were stern but kind. She remembered that look... Sophia closed her eyes and took a deep breath. She could hear the rustle of the wind, birds, the dogs panting nearby... then she heard Ulrich's respiration... her heartbeat... little by little she left the sounds behind and found stillness. In her mind, she saw the pots as they were and as they had been; two images, superimposed. She focused on the cleaned image... she drew that image out, until it became the dominant image and there was not other in her mind. She exhaled slowly and opened her eyes.

Ulrich nodded appreciatively. Iksha, Edgardo and Josh also nodded and smiled. There they were; the cleaned pots.

"Let's walk." Ulrich said, and he held Sophia by the elbow. All of a sudden she was back in the room with the sun and the stars. She looked around in confusion. She was alone in the theater and the screen was blank. She stood up and looked around. There was row after row of steep steps, that curved around a convex screen.

So that's how we get the impression of 3D, she said to herself, since she was there by herself... or was she? She looked towards the lower rows, where exits should have been and there was Ulrich. He was dressed in heaver clothes, just like she was. *It is cold here,* she thought.

Ulrich climbed the steps and joined her. "Yes, it is colder here." He smiled.

They both sat, then he motioned for her to look at the screen. There was their mountain, the shelf and Josh, Edgardo and Iksha moving to their positions.

"Where are we?" She turned to Ulrich.

He sighed and said that it was difficult to explain, then asked her to guess. He then turned to the screen and began to draw shapes in the air with his index finger.

"In the ether?" she said half jokingly.

He shook his head from side to side. "We could call it that... It is not a specific place, as much as a when." he said, while he continued to do motions with his finger.

Sophia's eyes widened with recall. "We are at the point where two dimensions cross..." Ulrich looked at her and smiled. On the screen she saw how, through Ulrich's finger motions, the excavation for the foundation took place.

She continued, "This is a graphical representation so that I may feel comfortable. I shared this image with Iksha, Edgardo and others, who will join us later... I shared other images also... a garden with a pond." she then stopped and turned to Ulrich. "I didn't share these images with Josh... that is why he has not mentioned the room with the sun and the stars. That is why we have different types of dreams."

"Uhum" Ulrich nodded but didn't contribute.

Sophia looked at the screen again. There they were, herself and Ulrich, sitting on top of boulders with the view of the shelf below. "Our bodies continue through the motions, even as part of ourselves is here..."

"Yes, what brought you here, just now?" Ulrich truly did not know.

"I remembered your eyes, the way you looked at me and the way you held my elbow. Why?" She asked.

"What else can you remember?" He asked in return.

Sighing, Sophia thought for a minute, as she continued to watch the screen. She saw Edgardo carve pieces of stone from their mountain and clump them together. He shaped the stones as if they were made of putty. He looked like a kid playing with a giant lump of playdoh.

"It is not a memory as much as a hunch... You are not from the same dimension as we are..." she said finally. Sophie felt sad.

Ulrich put one arm around her, pulled her to him and kissed her hair. "Just a couple of notes higher, Sophie..." He motioned for her to look at the screen. "I believe this is were we get to work." he said, with a slight hoarseness to his voice. "All we have to do is hold hands in that world and talk to each other..."

They held hands and watched as their images did the same. Ulrich and Sophie sat in the theater and talked about moving the stones. They both heard Edgardo, yell their names at the top of his lungs. They repressed laughter at Edgardo's surprised look when the first stone began to move. They talked about where Josh, Iksha and Edgardo were in relation to the stones. They alerted each other if they thought the stone should go higher. Little by little, they placed the stones and the foundation was laid.

It was mesmerizing to watch the castle take form. In the old world, Sophie had loved to build miniature models with her son and he had also loved to build online worlds with his friends. *I guess this is the way gamers felt...* Hours went by and Sophie vaguely registered that the afternoon sun was less bright.

"They need to rest, Sophie." Ulrich said, motioning towards Edgardo, who had just wiped his brow. All three, Iksha, Edgardo and Josh looked exhausted but Sophie felt great.

"Ulrich... you know we could do all this work by ourselves..." Sophie ventured.

"Yes... but our bodies would die. There would be the most beautiful castle and dry bones and skin left of us." he said with a grin.

"Is that true? Why?" She wanted to ask so much more.

"...because we are working in real time. What we usually call the soul, is eternal, but our bodies need nourishment. Today, we are just using something similar to telepathy to create an environment where we can both focus on the action."

"Ulrich, are me and Josh alive; are you real?"

He turned to her and began to say something, then thought better. "Yes, we are alive and I am as real as you are..." He finally said. "Now... wake up!"

Sophie came to herself on the path and her knees buckled. "Oh... my goodness..." she said as she looked for the ground. If it wasn't for Ulrich, who kept her from falling, she would have dropped on the spot.

"Uhum. You can feel it now." he said with a grin.

"You were not kidding!" Sophie felt sick to her stomach and very lightheaded.

Ulrich lowered her until they both sat on the ground.

"In time." He began, "You will remember how to draw energy from the environment. When we join the others you will see that, even though they didn't do physical work, Josh and Iksha are also very tired."

"Did we draw energy from them?" Sophie asked.

"You did." Ulrich said, matter of fact.

Sophie felt bad and immediately, apologetic, began to say that she would have never used them, had she known. Ulrich did not let her off the hook. "Sophie, you know these things already..."

Sophia stared at him hard. She felt anger raise up her throat. *How can he just sit there and tell me that I'm such a horrible person, then look so calm... so smug? No, he isn't smug.* He just looked at her, as if interested in her reaction. She forced herself to take a couple of deep breaths and went into her mind. She closed her eyes and focused on him. Feeling his energy, she found calm and... more calm. There was nothing deceitful about him.

"I don't like you very much right now." She finally said, frowning in mock chagrin.

Ulrich grinned and said. "I am sorry."

Well, at least I know that angels do have a sense of humor. She surprised herself at the thought. *Ulrich is not an angel; those things do not exist, unless... the myth began because of a misconception. What if angels were only more awakened humans? What if the assisted humans just didn't know what to make of these other types of humans? Here I go again... stop it!* Her mind had a way to going off into tangents and this was not the moment for contemplation.

As if reading her mind, or maybe because he did, Ulrich stood up and pulled her to her feet. "Let's go, Sophie. We need to help the others with dinner. Now, you can pull energy from the environment."

Her ego wanted to protest but her mind knew that he was right. She took several deep breaths. Sophie closed her eyes and, in her mind, she saw the green of the trees... the sky...so blue... the land. The land extended below her in majestic patches of color. The path stretched in front of her, soft and dappled with color. At the lowest levels, the ground pulsated with life. Sophie saw and felt, everything, at the same time. Her mind began to expand and she felt a tingling sensation all over her body. Her body felt lighter. She felt a swelling of emotion in her chest. Her heart filled with love at the beauty around her. She loved; she generated love towards all creation.

Sophie allowed her heart to fill with the energy of love until it flowed, and then, she allowed that love to burst in waves. The waves expanded and bathed everything with light. She allowed the expansion until she felt that her body could not handle anymore emotion. She would burst, dissolve and become part of all. She didn't burst and her heart did not explode. She reached crescendo then, gently cascaded down into calm.

Basking in the after glow, Sophie maintained her eyes closed, until she became aware of her surroundings again. Sophie opened her eyes; she felt good. She turned to Ulrich. The look in his eyes, wrapped her in pleasure. Ulrich stood transfixed, staring at her. He swallowed, before saying: "That was... good."

Sophie knew that, in some way, he had felt what she had felt. "You are a good teacher." she said and she gave him a winning smile. Sophie turned towards the shelf and sashayed off, before he could answer. Had she turned, she would have seen him, smile happy at her.

"Mom!"

Halted, Sophie turned and found her son riding downhill towards them. He looked positively drained but happy. *Oh my goodness... poor baby,* she thought; a pang of guilt returning. "Hi sweetie..." She called back.

Edgardo, not far behind, shook his head. "It was about time you called us. There better be a castle in that spot!" he said, half joking and half wishing.

Ulrich reached for Edgardo's horse and petted the beast. "I apologize that we kept you for so long. I think you will be pleased with the progress." he said, smiling up at Edgardo.

Sophie had been petting Bear, who never left the boy's side, when she heard the exchange. Ulrich hadn't told them everything. She felt growing respect towards his restraint. Had Ulrich told them, that they felt so tired because she had used their energy, the conversation would have become about Sophie. Attention remained on Edgardo and Josh, so that they received energy.

They walked, slowly, back to the camp. Edgardo and Josh, actually perked a little, when they began to talk about the moving stones. Josh related how Edgardo molded the stones...

"Like a big kid with playdoh." he said, echoing his mother's previous thoughts. "It was rad watching those things go up in the air, as if an invisible crane was lifting them!"

They were about to turn back to the shelf, when Ulrich motioned for them to wait. "Someone is coming." he said.

Sophia, followed his gaze and went into her heart. She sensed the environment around them; there was additional life. It's progress up their mountain could be traced as the forest creatures became aware of it. A couple of minutes later, they saw a horse drawn cart with two figures on the seat.

"Right on schedule." Josh said softly.

Sophia turned to her son. *This boy knows a lot more than he says...* She smiled to herself. It was true; things and people had shown at different intervals and just when they had needed them. She sighed deeply and said to herself, *one of us must have wished for something that we will need soon.*

The cart came to a stop near them. "Hello Sophia." A remarkable young woman greeted her warmly. Seated beside her, was a big oriental man.

"Hello, my name is Chul-Moo and this is Tamara." He introduced himself and his companion to the group.

Sophia smiled warmly at them. She could not remember them but their energy was good. Sighing, she told herself that she might as well get used to strangers greeting her like old friends. There was no way to tell how many souls she had met in the ether.

Ulrich came forward and petted one of their horses, while he said, "It is good to have you here. Was it the stone markers what showed you the path?"

Tamara and Chul-Moo exchanged an amazed look. "That, and when we saw stones flying through the air, we were pretty sure that this had to be the right place!" Chul-Moo said with exaggerated arm movements.

Edgardo laughed, "Ah, yes, that... " then he waited for Ulrich's queue.

Ulrich turned to Sophia, who nodded imperceptibly. "Let's go to the camp." he said, still looking at her, then he turned to the new arrivals. "There is a shower room there, I think you will enjoy."

"A shower!" Tamara said overjoyed, turning to Chul-Moo as if saying 'you see...'

Chul-Moo just smiled, pulled the reins and clicked his tongue to get the horses moving. "Just follow that way, right?" He asked, with arched eyebrows, to the other men as he nodded in the direction of the shelf.

"Yep. Yonder. We live yonder." said Josh. In time, the place would be known as Yonder Mount.

"Hello dears!" Iksha stood by the fire as perky as the last time they had seen her. "I have supper ready for you. It is simple food, but I hope to have a kitchen soon." Then she pointed to the construction. "It looks good, doesn't it?"

There it stood, about 200 yards from the cabin, a rectangular stone building. Edgardo and Josh were the first to touch the building. The model had given them an idea of how it would look but nothing could have prepared them for this.

After the awe wore off, Edgardo, stone carver by trade, trained a critical eye on it. "It is too simple... I needs more." he said.

"My dear, we almost have a house. This is most wonderful! You can decorate it later." Iksha appeased. "Now go wash; All of you, go wash."

The men used warm water from pails and washed outside, while Tamara and Sophie went to the shower room. On the way, Sophie told Tamara about herself and Josh; how they had found the cave and met the others. She began to explain the shower room. "It is not much. It is an opening in the cave, right under one of the water falls. We keep a fire burning, so that we can have warm water. We wash our clothes here and, sometimes, the water can get very cold..." her voice trailed off. Sophie had not seen the shower room since breakfast. "Edgardo!" He had been the last to join them for breakfast. *That sweet man...* she thought.

In front of them was, practically, an exotic spa. Edgardo, had carved a stone tub, seats and benches... even a raised fire pit. He had created private, enclosed areas with short walls. There was even a section of water fall, screened off by a half wall. Several people could tend to their personal hygiene, at the same time. He had left the walls of the cave, and most of the floor, natural. All that were missing were the large fluffy towels and scented oils and soaps.

Sophie showered, while Tamara took a bath. Sophie needed the cold water. Her nerves and senses felt overloaded. It had been less than a month, since they awoke at the meadow, and everyday there had been something new; a new lesson, synchronicity or person coming into her life. Sophie's preference, had always been to control sensory input. Part of her wanted to close her eyes and sleep for days. She remembered her dream, where the rider had smiled at her and given a thumbs up. Encouraged, she had allowed the storm to take her higher and she had experienced exhilaration. *Ok...* she said, to herself.

Tamara and Sophie approached the group. Ulrich was the first to notice them. Under the light of the fire, his eyes shone bright. He looked momentarily confused, then his face broke into an approving smile.

"New clothes?" He grinned, amused.

All eyes turned to them.

"Tamara has brought extra clothes for all of us." Sophie said, glad that darkness would conceal the warmth in her face. She had always, vaguely, perceived her beauty but had never been the type to intentionally attract attention.

"Oh my dears, you look beautiful." Iksha gushed. "I love gowns!" Tamara and Sophie wore simple, cap sleeve, long wrap dresses.

"Well, we can't call this a gown." Tamara had interjected. "In time, we will find ways to put our 'lady on'. I don't want to see those ugly trousers again." she said with comical emphasis. Tamara was a remarkable woman; tall with full lips and large almond eyes. Under the light of the fire, she looked burnished.

Sitting beside her son, Sophie turned to Iksha. "How come you have so much energy?"

"Aha... I know what you mean. I went to my garden, dear. I am most proud of my babies. I love them and they love me back!" Iksha beamed.

Nodding in appreciation, Sophie turned to Ulrich. "Yes, we can draw energy from the environment. Ulrich, would everyone draw energy, the same way?"

Ulrich, relaxed, resting on one elbow began to explain, "Each one of us has a particular activity that we love. Back in the old world, it was said to 'find something you love to do and you won't have to work a day in your life' Remember?"

They all nodded.

"Well, it is the same principle." Ulrich continued. "When we focus on something we love, such as Iksha with her plants, we give it the energy of love. Since energy can never be destroyed, only transformed, that energy returns to us multiplied."

"I can't be that simple... a thief loves to steal but it lands him in jail." Chul-Moo challenged.

Ulrich broke into a wide smile. "Yes, there is that... however, does the thief truly love to steal or does he love the challenge? If the thief rationalizes, in any way, what he does, then he makes excuses. Excuses are a way to justify guilt. Guilt is not of love. So we are back to the question. What does the thief truly love in the activity of stealing... see? That is why the activity may bring him material gain but not peace; not energy."

"There are some people, however, who do draw energy from hurting others..." Sophie said quietly.

"Yes..." Ulrich said, looking at her gently. "The old world functioned that way." They all stared at the fire for a moment.

Each and every one of them could mention an instance in which, they had either suffered or witnessed, an unethical act. They had all witnessed the product of unethical behavior, at all levels. There had been financial meltdowns, scandals, poverty, abuse, hate groups and much more. It was unnecessary to discuss the types and instances. They all felt good about their group. However, in the back of their minds, they all knew that the seed for greed had not died.

Josh broke the silence. "So... tell us, Chul-Moo and Tamara... what do you guys do?"

"I work with kunfell... metals." Chul-Moo said proudly.

"He doesn't work with metals... metals find him." Tamara jumped in. "This man... I thought we were never going to get here." She continued, shaking her head. "Every few steps, we would have to stop so 'Mo' here could 'listen for his little friends'..." she said, curving her index and middle fingers, into quotation signs.

Chul-Moo grinned wide, "Kunfell sings to me."

"Is that what you guys have on the back of that cart?" Josh asked.

"Yes, actually. There must be a ton of rock back there; I barely had any room left for my bags." Tamara said with wide open eyes.

"Rock or metal?" Josh frowned.

"Josh. The kunfell needs to be purified, you understand?" Chul-Moo began to explain.

"Don't tell me... you need fire for that. Very hot fire... Right?" Josh interjected.

"Yes." Chul-Moo answered simply.

Sophie smiled at her son, then turned to Ulrich. "They saw the stones up in the air..." She nodded towards Tamara and Chul-Moo. "...a forge could be even more visible... specially at night..."

Ulrich nodded and stared at her, then turned to Josh. "You know the risks."

Josh stared back at Ulrich. "It is going to happen, sooner or later."

Chul-Moo, who had followed the exchange, volunteered his opinion. "We could work in a cave. How far this one go?"

Neither Sophie nor Ulrich could answer. It had not occurred to them to sense beyond the walls.

"Maybe, I can look into that tomorrow." Edgardo offered. "Tonight, I am tired. Ladies... buenas noches." He stood up to leave, then turned. "You know... it is truly beginning to get crowded in that cave. I would like to finish the house first. I want a bed; a real bed, before I worry about melting ores."

They all smiled and bid him good night.

Sophie turned to Ulrich. "Could we finish the house without using metal?"

Ulrich smiled and said, "No hinges, door handles, water faucets, grid for cooking in the kitchen..."

"I'll talk to him." Iksha smiled and winked at them.

Tamara, Chul-Moo and Iksha excused themselves for the night, leaving Josh, his Mom and Ulrich to themselves.

"It is going to happen sooner or later?" She turned to Josh.

"Yes Mom. The marauders are becoming curious about the newcomers. They have sent scouts." Josh answered.

Sophie felt her heart sink. She had wished this new world would be different. "Maybe, we can help them. How civilized are they, Josh?" She asked hopeful.

"Hum." Josh nodded his head uncertain, then he continued. "There are actually two types of survivors, Mom. There is the group of marauders, who are not very civilized at all. They have weapons; knives, bows, rudimentary spears and mallets. Then, there is another group... these other guys look like something out of Raccoon City."

Sophie ignored Ulrich's puzzled look. "Ulrich." She turned a serious look to him. "What can you tell us."

Ulrich nodded. "I can tell you about the old world, the survivors and about the newcomers. There are some things that you already know but Josh does not."

"Ok." she said.

Ulrich summarized the story of the change. "You know that old earth became polarized, during the last days. There were groups who wanted peace, while there were other groups who wanted war. War was profitable. The groups who wanted war tried to take control of the communications apparatus. They knew that people could be controlled that way. Their idea was to separate people through hate.

There was hate of one religious group against another; hate of one ethnic group against another and even hate against anyone who had a little more than another. The groups who wanted peace, managed to keep the balance, until the cycling began.

There is a cycle of creation and destruction that takes place all through the universe. The cycle happens at different times for different worlds. When the time for Earth to go through one of these cycles came near, there were physical changes on earth and psychological changes in the population.

On earth, there were massive floods, earthquakes, volcanoes... everything that happens when tectonic plates move...fast. Leaders wanted to avoid massive panic in the population, so they said that rain had caused sinkholes, building collapses and floods. There had been very little rain, instead liquefaction is what flooded some areas. Leaders truly believed that they were acting in everyone's best interest.

There were several groups of people, who had studied the history of the world, and became aware of a pattern. You, Sophie, became aware of the pattern in religious texts. Thousands of years before you, other people had become aware of the same pattern. These people tried to alert the world but those who took over altered the texts, after the original leaders died. The original texts, which did not have religion in mind, had been written in languages that had been lost anyway, so it was easy for the new leaders to change words.

So, thousands of years later, we had a world in which the original knowledge of creation had been lost. There were many groups who spread the message that some would be saved and some would not. That message was, in part, true but the original message did not have anything to do with religious affiliation. There were groups who said that it would be aliens and that the aliens would save those who wanted to help others. That message also had an ingredient of truth.

Where all those teachers and prophets failed, was in the attitudes they taught people. People learned to look down on those who did not 'listen' to them. They felt superior to others, because they were prepared. Instead, they were the ones who actually carried the seed of destruction within.

They judged others. They rejected any possibility that their idea might not be 'the true path' as they called it. Their frustration, anger and pride contributed to the energy that already polluted the planet. They believed they were right, so their vibration attracted situations that would prove them right.

Those who expected hardship, encountered a cataclysm, survived and experienced terrible hardship. Those who had set aside goods and weapons and expected anarchy... that's what they saw... Eventually, the original survivors died. Languages were mixed, knowledge lost and the descendants... they have a corrupted memory. The massive cataclysms destroyed and buried structures and the rest, was claimed by vegetation. Even the pyramids are gone. The map of earth has changed."

Ulrich paused to see if he had lost them, so Sophie and Josh nodded encouragement. "The newcomers... Back in the days before the cataclysm, there were many kind people. These people rejected what they were told by the media, governments and religious organizations. That was the key.

There were people on earth, of all religious backgrounds and beliefs, who felt sadness at the thought of people dying; any people, not just their people. They did not share their opinions with anyone, specially people from their own religious affiliation. Each and every one of these people said one day: 'let it be thy will' They released control to the divine. Little did they know that in doing so, they allowed their own higher selves to come through.

They did not sit and watch for the end of the world. They did not keep score about who would be saved and who would not. At first, they felt pain. There was emotional pain and later physical pain. Some people called it the 'vibrational flu' Several discovered, later, that their intuition had grown. These people could practically read other's minds. Many changed jobs, got divorces, moved, in short, they left the past behind. Many of them are here now and many more will come."

"Wait... you said that the original survivors died. Where have we been all this time?" Josh asked frowning. "The math doesn't work."

"Aha... that's when the aliens come in." Ulrich smiled. "I think you have heard of the term 'folding space' before. The aliens pushed at the membrane of their dimension and allowed you to touch on it; that sucked you out of there. It's similar to when a bubble of air, in water, meets another bubble... a little push and they become one... Your bodies were kept in stasis, while your consciousness interacted with them and other newcomers. It had to be done that way because we had to allow time for the earth to heal."

Now it was Sophie's turn to ask a question. "Ulrich, you say that ~*we*~ were kept in stasis... where were you all this time?"

Ulrich stared at her. "That, I cannot tell you."

"Well, how convenient..." Sophie retorted.

Ulrich laughed good naturedly. "I am sorry." he said, with a twinkle in his green eyes. He stood up and said, "It is time to get rest." before Sophie and Josh realized that they had many more questions.

10

ABOUT TAMARA, LOVE AND ANGER

Breakfast conversation centered around the castle. It was decided that Josh and Chul-Moo would search for a suitable site to set up a forge; Sophie and Ulrich would scan the landscape for downed trees and help Edgardo inspect the cave. They were to meet, back at the fire, in about two hours. Iksha planned to tend to her flock, garden and prepare meals.

"I guess I could help Iksha..." Tamara offered.

Sophie smiled and asked, "What did you before?"

"I was a database manager, but there are no computers here."

"Well, eventually we will need a records keeper... What did you love to do?" Sophie continued probing.

Tamara raised her eyebrows and with a glint in her eyes said, "I loved to shop for clothes."

"Uhum... and you were the one who got the extra clothes for us." Sophie smiled, then turned to Iksha. "Could your babies tell us which ones would be good for making thread?"

Iksha's eyes sparkled with understanding, "Yes, I will most definitely ask them. Then take Tamara to where she can find them."

"Let me know if you go anywhere past the lake, please. Just call my name and I will hear you." Sophie instructed, without going into details. When the others had left, Sophie turned to Ulrich. "I don't see why you and me can't make the metal parts."

Ulrich saw right through her, "Sophie... you know why... we can't interfere with free will."

"I can't wish to protect my son?" Sophie challenged.

"How will he discover his potential?" Ulrich asked, patiently.

Stubborn, Sophie turned to go to the cave, but Ulrich held her back. "We should meet at the screening room."

"We told Edgardo we would go with him." Sophie countered.

"We can do that from the screening room." He insisted.

Sophie felt the need to get away from him but there was too much work left to do. "Ok." she said.

They found their usual spot and sat in front of each other. Ulrich guided them through a recognition of the surrounding areas, then into the screening room. "Hallo." he said good naturedly.

"Uhum." Sophie nodded.

He took a long look at her, then asked, "Do you remember when I said that we should be careful about our thoughts?"

Sophie immediately saw herself through his eyes. "Forgive me. I am not as... advanced as you are yet."

"What is truly bothering you, Sophie?" He ignored the poke.

"I am not sure... the marauders... life is not perfect here... you." She enumerated.

Ulrich nodded, then he pointed towards the images on the screen. "Each and everyone of them has abilities. If we were to do everything for them, we would deprive them of the means to grow."

"...and we would be miserable because we would feel their longing... in time their eyes would be opened and they would realize that we had actually been selfish. I wish for them to be safe so that I do not have to worry. I know..." she said, lowering her eyes.

"Why do I bother you?" Ulrich asked, smiling now.

"...because I feel a connection with you but, at the same time, a disconnect." She was honest. "I can't read you... Why are you here? "

"There is a connection and a disconnect. I can't read you, sometimes, either and I am here because I chose to be." He answered in order.

Edgardo had found a weakness in the wall, so Sophie and Ulrich had to turn their attention to him. They communicated to him that they could see him and that they would hold falling stones, should there be any. Edgardo began to carve out the rock. After a while, he found another chamber, which he began to explore, under the light of a torch. Meanwhile, Josh and Chul-Moo had found another cave near the top water fall.

"Does that cave feel solid to you Ulrich? Would it be a good place for a forge?" Sophie asked.

Ulrich took a moment, before answering. "That cave, will eventually connect to ours below. The walls are solid. It would be as good a place as any other. We are on a mountain. The fires will be seen at night regardless. Even the camp fire can be seen, Sophie."

"I know..." She knew she could not stop life; every action had a reaction and so on...

Instead of meeting at the camp, Ulrich communicated the images to the whole group. Everyone understood that Edgardo was to make a way to the cave where Josh and Chul-Moo were; that Ulrich would begin to create timbers and Sophie would move them. Tamara and Iksha were free to continue their explorations.

Everyone went about their stated chores for the day. Sophie stayed in the screen room by herself, since Ulrich needed to move about the mountains to find pieces of wood. From her vantage point, Sophie could see the comings and goings of her son, Tamara and Iksha, Ulrich and even Edgardo. In reality, her body sat on a flat boulder, above the main cave.

Sophie moved stones, when Edgardo called from inside the cave and timbers, when Ulrich finished forming them.

Edgardo carved another chamber inside their mountain, with passageways and steps leading into the other cave. Ulrich created timbers, taller and thicker than existing trees, to support the roof of the building. She still did not feel comfortable calling it castle; it sounded pretentious but her son loved the term. She sighed, *there could be worse things.*

They worked for hours, until Ulrich came into the screen room. "Hallo..." He greeted as he sat beside her.

"Is it time to take a break?"

"I think so. Iksha has cooked dinner and she does not like to wait." he said smiling.

Sophie finished carrying a batch of stones out of the cave, then pointed towards Josh and Chul-Moo. "That boy has been having the time of his life discovering how hot he can make that fire. The stone tub Edgardo made for them works well."

Ulrich looked at Josh on the screen for a while. "He needs to be careful. He can get that fire hotter than necessary. Fire like that can burn through anything."

"Uhum." said Sophie, not fully understanding but perceiving Ulrich's concern. "Should we talk to him?" She then asked.

He turned to her, she had used the word 'we' had she remembered? "I... am open." He finally said, noncommittal.

Sophie noticed the pause and felt his hesitation. She took it for reluctance to get involved. Something inside of her retreated. "Ok. Let's take a break." she said, more upbeat than she felt. She became aware of her surroundings and stood up. Ulrich, beside her, looked concerned. Sophie felt anger raise up her throat and turned to the return path. She could not understand herself. Her rational mind told her that there was no reason for her to resent him. *Why does he have to be so... perfect?*

Ulrich, who had walked silent beside her, held her arm and stopped her. "Sophie, we need to center ourselves, before we join the others. Your anger will change the mood of the camp."

She gave him a side glance and blinked. There was something in his eyes that she had not seen before. It almost looked like anger. *What is he angry about?*

"I am far from perfect." he said, letting her know that he could read her mind.

"I thought you said that you could not read me." She reproached.

"Not all the time." He reminded her.

Ulrich began to glow. Sophie blinked. It was still a new experience to see auras. His glow extended towards her, then back to him. She felt anger, betrayal, loss... The more she focused on the emotion, the greater it became. Sophie could not ignore his eyes anymore. They were fierce. It was as if he felt the same as she did. Then it dawned on her that he did feel the same. It was a feedback loop. He was her mirror. *Well, how about that...* she thought. Sophie forgot about the emotion and became interested in the dynamics of the interaction. She became an observer. Both their bodies glowed.

"You know we should stop them before someone gets hurt, right?" Ulrich said, beside her.

Sophie realized that both, her and Ulrich, had become spectators. "What is exactly happening there?" Sophie asked, with detached curiosity.

"It is the ego or memory of the body, Sophie. Your memories of rejection are fresh." he said.

"Hum... Why is your aura attacking me?" She asked.

"That's the way it first looked, from your perspective, in reality our auras have been in touch all along. You noticed it, just now, because your anger... grew. Ego feeds on the energy of others, so it sought energy from me. I am allowing the energy to drain from me, then I take yours. That was the way of the old world." Ulrich explained.

Sophie remembered all that she had read about power struggles and realized that if Ulrich had not allowed her to take his energy, she would have drained and contaminated the others. Moods are contagious. Then, Sophie's memories came back; she remembered.

"You did not reject me. I needed to remember our connection." Sophie said quietly.

"Should we save these two bodies from further damage?" Ulrich proposed.

Sophie came to herself and felt tired. "I chose to forget because I thought that I had caused you pain. I am the one who remembers the pain of rejection. You have surpassed that stage." Sophie remembered how Ulrich had chosen to follow her. She could have jumped to his level, but she was too attached to her son... and this world.

Ulrich smiled, then he pulled her to himself. They embraced for a long time. When they finally separated, Sophie asked, "What happened? I mean, I remember what happened with me. I... basically told them... to forget it, but you?"

Ulrich grinned. Fresh from the third dimension, Sophie's language had been much more colorful. "You told them a little more than that." He looked at her, then his eyes became distant with recall. He finally added, "You could say that I took advantage of a wrinkle in time."

"I thought you guys were above all that... you know, impatience." she said.

"Sophie... our level is still so... young. There are so many levels..." Ulrich said, smiling gently at her, then, with a glint in his eyes, he added, "I hear that even the higher-up guys get frustrated at the rules."

11

A LITTLE SURPRISE

They found Iksha by the fire. "You know dear..." She began, looking at Ulrich, "I would really like to have a table..." Iksha had been placing the food on a square of tarp, on the ground. "Your babies are good, but I think they would sneak a bite, if I turn my back on them." she said, pointing at Bear and Termite, who laid at a distance like sphinxes, watching her every move.

Sophie smiled and asked, "Is Josh back? We didn't see them on the path."

"Ah yes, they came down through the stairs that Edgardo made for them. It is most wonderful what he has done in that cave." She smiled satisfied. "All three of them are in the shower room. They said, that they had worked harder than any of us, today, and they deserved to wash inside. There might be some hot water left for you, Ulrich."

Ulrich nodded and moved towards the cave. "I'll make tables and chairs for you Iksha." He called over his shoulder.

Sophie sat down on one of the flat boulders; Bear and Termite came, tails gently wagging, to get their lovings. "Where is Tamara?" She asked.

"I think she went to the lake. Tamara said she wanted to look for clay and grasses." Iksha said, as she handed Sophie a cup of tea.

"Thank you, Iksha. The building is coming along nicely, isn't it? Is there anything, different from the model, that you would like us to add?"

Iksha stood, with one hand on a hip, and looked up at the building. "Well, the kitchen is big... I see now that the roots would have to go in the basement; it is cold down there... I think the herb room should have a window, for fresh air but the storage needs to be protected from the outside. I would like to see glass; we need light and to keep bugs away. Oh, and I don't want to walk too far to the dining room." She added frowning. "I overheard Ulrich say that the big room, near the front, would be the great hall...? That is too far from the kitchen."

Sophie nodded. "I agree. I think he means it as a general hall. A place for meetings. There is more people coming and, eventually, the kitchen dining may be too small." She reasoned.

"Hello Ladies!" Tamara greeted as she sat beside Sophie. "Well, aren't you the sneaky one..." She told Sophie.

"Hum?" Sophie smiled, confused and raised one eyebrow.

"I saw you and Ulrich on the path..." Tamara winked at her. "I thought you two were all spiritual and shit..."

Nonplussed, Sophie opened her mouth to say something but stopped and just shook her head.

"It's all right dear; she's just envious." Iksha said, smiling broadly and winking at Tamara.

"Girl... haven't you seen that man? That's OK... I have my Mo." Tamara said with a thin smile. Tamara was quiet for a moment, then, remembering what she had seen, she became animated again. "How come you haven't kissed that man? All I saw, was a whole lotta hugging but no kiss! What's up with that?"

"Tamara!" Iksha mock scolded, "The woman must make the man wait."

Sophie was certain that her face was going to spontaneously ignite. Finally, she said, "It's complicated." Then she grabbed a pail of hot water and went to the washstand that Iksha had set for the men, the night before.

Relentless, Tamara followed her. "You know he likes you..."

"Tamara... " Sophie decided to nip it in the bud. "Thank you." she said, then she gave Tamara, a crazy hard stare, girl code for 'don't go there.' Sophie wished that she could allow herself to giggle with the girls but she had more pressing issues in her mind.

Unfazed, Tamara was about reply, when they heard voices and laughter coming from the cave. The men, washed and changed into the new clothes, poured out.

"Hello." Josh called to his Mom, with a big smile on his face.

"Hi sweetie." Sophie called back, taking advantage of the distraction, to get away from Tamara. "You look good."

"Yes, you all do..." Tamara said and flashed knowing eyebrows to Sophie.

"Yes, I look good; how you like me now, baby." said Chul-Moo, as he put an arm around Tamara's waist.

Tamara gave him a winning smile and walked away with him. They all sat by the fire and had an animated conversation about their day. Josh was the most excited.

"Mom, you have to see it. I can get that fire white hot." he said.

"That is amazing. Just with intention?" Sophie smiled thinking of how crazy this world was. She then remembered Ulrich's earlier comment and added, "Sweetie, be careful... We don't want to melt our mountain."

"Aw... that can't happen..." Josh said, then remembering where they were, turned to Ulrich, "...right?"

Ulrich nodded, thankful for the opportunity to discuss the subject, "We have developed our abilities to a certain degree. Once we become comfortable with this level, it is natural that we will want to explore and see how much more we can do. Josh, now you use fire that has already been lit and expand it. Soon, you will see that you can increase the vibration in any object, to create fire. That's when the danger comes; be mindful of how much you increase that rate. You don't want to go past a certain threshold. If you release the energy, without taking precautions, you could hurt all of us."

Josh thought a minute then asked, "You mean like an atomic bomb?"

Ulrich nodded. "Something like that..."

Josh let out a long whistle. "I had no idea..."

"Uhum, That's why we must remember to allow people to discover their abilities, on their own. When they ask, we teach, otherwise, we observe and guide. If they don't ask, then we must keep a watchful eye and be prepared to avert disaster." Ulrich said, looking around at the group, then resting his eyes on Sophie.

They sat in silence, considering the implications of what Ulrich had disclosed. Tamara noticed the exchange between Sophie and Ulrich and understood. That is why these two can't relax, she thought to herself. She had felt put-off, earlier, when Sophie had refused to have fun with the girls but now she felt bad. She smiled apologetically to Sophie, then Chul-Moo broke the silence. He turned to Edgardo and asked him if he could make molds for him.

"What type of molds?" Edgardo asked.

"I need to make tools." Chul-Moo said then, he remembered where they were and turned to Ulrich. "Hold on... couldn't I create the tools with intention? Could you teach me?"

"Chul-Moo, you can create the tools with intention." Ulrich said then, he added. "First, allow your mind to ponder the problem. What must the tool do. Visualize the feel, weight and size. Trust in the process and the right tool will materialize. Of course, make sure that you have a chunk of metal in front you first. Eventually, you will mold metal the same way that Edgardo molds stone."

Iksha jumped in. "My dear, let me know when you begin to make tools because I have a couple of items to order. I need more pots... big pots for my kitchen."

They laughed good naturedly. Iksha was determined to stock her kitchen well. It truly would be her kitchen, since she had declared it so.

"Do we have any idea of when will we get more people and how much they know?" Iksha asked.

Josh turned to his Mom. "You haven't had nightmares in a couple of days, right?"

"Come to think of it... no." Sophie could not remember any dreams since the meadow.

"We probably have a couple of days." he said, then added. "We had dreams, before you came here. We haven't since."

Sophie remembered the crowd in the screen room and turned to Ulrich. "Is everyone in the screen room coming here or have they been dispersed through the planet?"

Ulrich nodded and proceeded to brief them. "Dispersed. There are many other sites being built on the planet. We all chose each other and created groups. The first group, is the builders. The next group continues the work with teachers, healers, crafts people, suppliers and so on. That's the group of people from the garden, Sophie."

Josh frowned, "Teachers? Aren't you and my Mom the teachers?"

Ulrich smiled, "Teachers of men, Josh... There will be the need for a common language, record keeping and sharing of information; Schools, Josh."

Josh sighed, "Hope they're better than some of the teachers I had..."

They finished dinner and chores then went back to the cave. It had been a busy day. Each one needed to process all the inputs of the day.

"One more night on this hard floor." Edgardo said.

Sophie smiled, and watched him turn in for the night. She reached above her head and ruffled her son's hair. "Good night sweetie." she whispered.

Ulrich, watched her from the other side of the room. She turned to look at him. He rested on one elbow with one leg raised, bent at the knee. She ran her eyes down his body. In spite of the baggy clothes, his masculine beauty came through.

Tamara was right... she thought as she drifted off to sleep.

Sophie woke up with a start. The Termite stood watching her sleep, practically breathing into her face, like she did when she wanted her mistress to wake up. She raised herself on one elbow and looked around the room. Ulrich's place was empty and so was Josh's. None of the men where in their spots. She closed her eyes and listened for movement. There was the faint mumble of voices, coming from outside the cave.

What are these guys up to now? She wondered, as she petted her little gray guardian. She stood up to go outside and noticed that, further beyond, the cave turned into something like a tunnel. *What on earth...?* Slowly, to keep from waking the other ladies, Sophie approached the entrance of the cave. Instead of the outside, there was a hallway lighted by something like torches, at either side. She felt apprehension constrict her chest. *Is this a dream or another dimension? If so, since when did the dogs began to come with me?* In the middle of her sleepy reasonings, she heard Ulrich in her mind, "It's Ok, Sophie." Relieved, she continued down the hallway.

Ulrich was already coming to meet her from the other end. "Hallo, I am sorry we woke you up." he said, beaming to her. "But, since you are up, come, let me show you." He looked very happy and excited.

The hallway opened into a room with doors to either side. Ulrich guided her, through the door on the right, and she found herself in the kitchen. "Oh my..." Sophie said with delight.

The kitchen was huge. There was enough room for two fireplaces. One fireplace sat on the same wall as the door from which they had just entered. Sophie had never seen a fireplace design like this one. The hearth area looked like a shallow stone tub with a cavernous hood over it. It had been placed at about three feet off the ground and covered an area of about two feet deep by four feet wide.

This hearth had been designed as a grill to cook with wood charcoal. It had enough room to place several pots and pans, at the same time, over the fire. Hooks and racks on brackets would hold these pots at different heights, to achieve different temperatures. There were even hooks to hang a spit.

At both sides of the grill, sat little ovens, with fire boxes below. Smooth new wood paddles, with long handles, hung from the wall at the sides of each oven. The wood bin, was built-in with grid shelves, so that the wood would stay dry. On one side of the wood bin, there was a rack with ash scoops, pokers and a small, long handle broom.

Across from the cooking area, sat a good size work island. It's surface was a two inch thick slab of deep green marble with gold specks in it. It was supported by a central stone pillar and corner columns. Below, there were shelves with plenty of room for storage. A rack, laden with pots and pans hanging from hooks, hovered above.

Counters, cupboards and doors lined one side wall. The opposite wall hosted the wet area. A long slab of tan stone had been carved in the shape of two beautiful farm house sinks, with drain grooves at either side. Above the sinks, there were windows and wood slat shelves to allow for air drying of utensils. Below the slab, which was also supported by stone pillars, shelves provided more storage area.

Beyond the work table was an eight seat dining table and, on the wall opposite to the cooking area, sat the other fireplace. This one looked more like the fireplaces that Sophie had seen before. It, clearly, had been designed for gathering around the fire. A simple stone mantle surrounded the hearth and there was a wood shelf above. There were chairs and little side tables, positioned at either side of the hearth.

Sophie was besides herself in awe. This kitchen would have made any cook happy, even in the old earth. "Iksha is going to love this..."

"I hope so." Edgardo said, apologetic. "I haven't the chance to add the details yet..."

"Oh, Edgardo, are you kidding? This kitchen would have cost a fortune, back in old earth. This is amazing... look at this sink... and we have running water!" Sophie said, still in awe.

Sophie would have gladly stayed and admired the kitchen for hours. There were so many useful details. *Such an intuitive design...* Ulrich realized that, at their current pace, daybreak would come before Sophie was finished exploring the rest of the castle.

"Come, there is more." Ulrich he said, pulling her by the hand.

The kitchen opened to a dining room with two long tables. There were was a long buffet table on one side of the room and a plate cupboard on the other side. The furniture pieces were massive, unlike anything she had seen before. Next to the dining room, was the entrance hall. The entrance hall opened to the main hall and to a sitting room. Ulrich walked her through the rooms like a tour guide. He explained the function of the room, told her a couple of anecdotes, then moved her to the next.

Sophie lingered in the main hall. Her eyes traveled up the wood stairs, to the gallery above and finally to the two story ceiling. She then noticed the fireplace hood and the hearth, at the opposite end of the room. There was a sitting area, next to the fireplace, dining tables and chairs on the sides of the room and plenty of open floor in the middle. This was not a main hall; this was a ballroom!

Sophie ran her hand over the wood of the doors, gallery support columns and furniture. "Ulrich, you guys have been up all night..." She turned to him. There were iron details everywhere. "The fires..."

He looked at her and opened his mouth to say something, but thought better of it. Instead, he pulled her outside with the Termite trailing close behind. They walked a few paces, before thick fog enveloped them. Neither the edge of the shelf, nor the land below, could be seen.

"It covers the whole mountain." Ulrich said.

Shivering, Sophie sighed and turned to him relieved. "Did you do that?" she asked with hunched shoulders, hugging herself. The fog had shrouded the castle but also dropped the temperature considerably.

"The guys would not wait and I knew that you would not forgive me if the marauders saw the fires." he said quietly. He wrapped both arms around her and turned her to face the mountain. "Look..." he said. Neither the fires, in the upper cave, nor much of the building could be seen. "They can't be seen against the mountain, even if the lights are on inside. It has shutters and a slate roof. It is a good building." he said, satisfied, then continued, "The bedrooms are above. We piped the water from the upper lake into the cave. One pipe goes to the water heater, and the other, goes into the castle. We used gravity to feed the water to all the faucets. The water comes from above, we use it, then the waste runs below into the septic system. We build it like you told us, but bigger... much bigger."

Back inside the building, Ulrich resumed his tour guide pace. He showed her the bedrooms. There were bedrooms with private baths and those that shared one in the hallway. There were rooms for every activity necessary to provide for the inhabitants of a huge household. There was furniture in every room; high beds with frames for canopies, armories, trunks, desks and chairs.

Running her hand over a desk, an almost intimidating piece of solid wood, Sophie turned in awe. "Ulrich... this is amazing... how did you guys get this done in such a short time?"

He nodded and explained: "We joined intention. I knew that we would not be able to finish, if we worked the old way, so I helped develop their intention."

They found Josh, laying on a bed in one of the rooms, with the Bear stretched by his side. "Hey Mom... like my room?" He beamed at her. "We used all those feathers you have been collecting... Ulrich sanitized them...multiplied them.... He also made these giant bags to put them in... the sheets... all this stuff." he said, stretching on the bed.

Sophie sat next to her son. "It really is not a bad mattress. I bet Edgardo is going to love this..."

"Oh, he does... he almost fell asleep, earlier." Ulrich told them.

"Should we wake up the ladies and bring them here?" Sophie asked.

"Sure. Your room has a front view. Wanna see?" Josh took off with both dogs scrambling to keep pace with him.

Sophie's room was next to his. He opened the windows and the shutters. It was dark outside, so there was not much to see. "Oh, I forgot the fog."

"It's OK sweetie. Why don't you go get some rest?" Sophie said and hugged her son. She watched her son go, followed by his canine guardians, into his room. She turned to Ulrich and asked him if he was coming with her.

"It is not necessary. The guys have already gone to get their ladies." Ulrich said.

"Oh... I didn't know that Edgardo and Iksha had... spoken." Sophie said surprised.

Ulrich raised an eyebrow at her.

"...but they did... before coming into this world." Sophie added.

"Uhum." Ulrich nodded.

Sophie felt suddenly very tired. "Ulrich... I can't remember everything we talked, back in the ether and right now... I just don't..."

Ulrich repressed a smile and simply said, "Let's go to sleep."

Ulrich laid down first and pulled her to him. He cradled her with one arm, while he caressed her arm with the other. Sophie realized that the touch of his skin was familiar. Ulrich buried his head in her hair and pressed her to him. Sophie closed her eyes and allowed her senses to take over. His body, warm and firm, molded just right to her curves. She loved his smell, clean with a hint of the woods. Sophie fell asleep thinking of how much she loved to be there with him.

12

ULRICH'S MISTAKE

It was late into the morning, when Sophie awoke. Sunlight, coming through the window, hurt her eyes. *We will have to make curtains... This is ridiculous.* She thought to herself, as she rubbed sleepy off her eyes. Ulrich was not in the room, so she figured he had gone downstairs. She laid back on the bed and remembered the night before.

That was nice. Then, with a deep sigh, she got up. This room had a private bath room. "Hum... nice; won't have to walk too far in the winter." she said to herself.

The bathroom had a tub, facilities and even a dressing area. *and there are mirrors.* Sophie caught her reflection and sighed. "That is... sad." she said, shaking her head. Her hair, naturally curly, was in full rebellion. "I look like a skinny mop..." she said aloud. She had lost a lot of weight since the last time she had seen her reflection on a mirror. *At least, I still have a profile...*

Sophie decided that it was time to love herself a little. She took a hot bath and manifested scented oils for her body and hair. Once dry, back at the mirror, she ran her fingers through her hair, visualizing long, silky waves. Satisfied with the result, she was about to work on her dress but changed her mind. *Hum... better wait.* She tied her hair with a strip of leather and left to join the others.

Meanwhile by the cabin, Ulrich and Chul-Moo were putting the finishing touches to the new horse stable. They had turned the cabin into a work shop and tool storage and, beside it, they had created the stable. The mountain shelf was large enough that there was room for the stable, barns, the main house and even a vegetable garden. To either side of the shelf, there were paths. One lead to the orchard, while the other, to the upper lake and the forge.

Josh caught up with the guys and congratulated them on the work done. He, then, turned to Ulrich. "You have a minute?" Josh asked, indicating that he wanted to have a private conversation with the man.

Ulrich sensed that Josh did not feel as lighthearted as he appeared. "Certainly." he said then, he followed the boy.

As they walked towards the house, Josh said, "I saw you come out of my Mother's room this morning."

Ulrich gave Josh a side glance. Josh stood shoulder to shoulder with him and weighted, probably, just as much. However, Ulrich did not sense any animosity. "Yes." He answered, simply.

"You have to tell her." Josh said, without preamble.

Ulrich stopped and stared at Josh. Of the many things he still needed to tell Sophie, which one could the boy mean? Then it dawned on him; Josh could see... "Josh... what happened with Sabrina was..." Ulrich began to say.

"Not your fault, I know." Josh interrupted. "...yet, you carry guilt."

Ulrich took a long look at Josh. *This boy knows more than what he says.* He nodded. "I will talk with Sophie." They were almost at the front door, when Ulrich turned to Josh. "Other than that... are you OK with us..."

Josh grinned and said, "Hum... yeah. Be good to her. You don't want to get on her bad side."

Ulrich smiled back. He wondered if Josh knew how true that statement was. "That bad?" he asked the boy, as a way to make conversation.

Josh looked distant for a moment, then he said, "Not really. It used to be bad... when she worked and had to spend a lot of time at work. I could take the lectures. It was the hurt in her eyes, when she looked disappointed..."

Ulrich patted him on the shoulder. "Trust that hasn't happened in a long time..."

"Nah... I didn't use to like school much... but then, something happened that I started liking it. I got good grades and I never saw that look again." Josh smiled and shrugged his shoulders.

They found Edgardo giving the finishing touches to a carved moulding around the entrance to the main hall. He had been busy all morning adding decorations to the foyer. There were carved niches, mouldings and lintels.

"That looks good, Edgardo." Josh said, as he ran his fingers over the stone.

"It's nothing... there is so much more I want to do." Edgardo said, humbly, as he looked around the room.

Ulrich smiled thinking that Edgardo could spend a lifetime carving the stones and still find more to do. "We're on our way to the kitchen." He told the man.

"As a matter of fact, so was I." Edgardo stood up and, resolute, marched ahead of them.

Josh and Ulrich followed behind, smiling at how quickly Edgardo had responded to the word 'kitchen.'

Iksha looked radiant. She moved from the grill to the work island, as she issued instructions to Sophie and Tamara. "We will have a proper supper now." She smiled, satisfied.

The little dynamo had worked all morning in setting up her kitchen. Tamara had helped her bring the bags from the cave, while the others were away. They had separated the supplies and added fresh vegetables. Iksha's love for the plants, had been returned with abundance.

"Ulrich, I will need your assistance in procuring meats for the winter. We must test our food preservation skills. We will also need a smoker." She instructed.

Obedient, Ulrich nodded, as him and Josh washed their hands. They knew better than to sit at her table with dirty hands. Iksha was even more of a stickler for hygiene, than Sophie. They were supposed to wash their hands before sitting down to eat and after petting any of the animals.

Chul-Moo came in and sat at the kitchen dining table. "Mo, go wash. You have been out there, with those horses." Iksha pointed a knife at him.

"Yah, ajuma." he said, as he stood up grinning and both hands on the surrender.

They chose the smaller dining, instead of the main hall, to set up the table. It truly looked beautiful with golden bread, rice and chicken dishes, green salad, fruit and berry tarts. There also was juice, tea and water to drink. Iksha looked at the table satisfied and nodded. "That is how we should eat." she said.

Seated at the table, they looked at each other. There was a momentary pause, as they all felt that something needed to be said. "Thank you for a wonderful meal, Iksha. Thank you to everyone for the work in creating this house. May we continue to learn and share in our abilities." Josh said, finally.

After lunch and chores, Tamara and Sophie went to the sewing room. Sophie explained to Tamara how she created through visualization. "I begin by studying the material. If I can, I use a model. In this case, we could use threads from the tarp. Study the thread until you can see it clearly in your mind. It will feel a little funny... in your head. For me, it feels as if my brain is swelling. There is no pain, just something like tingling and pressure."

Tamara followed Sophie's instructions and soon, she was manifesting thread. Then she moved to manifesting thread of different colors and textures. She learned to multiply the material and weave it.

"This is actually... fun. Who would have thought." Tamara said, shaking her head.

When he felt it would be appropriate, Ulrich poked his head and asked Sophie to come with him.

"You go girl..." Tamara said, giving her an innocent look.

Ulrich smiled and winked at the girl, as he guided Sophie out of the room.

Ulrich guided Sophie in the direction of the front door. Once outside the house, he said, "Let's walk." They walked in comfortable silence until they reached the edge of the shelf. From this spot, they could see on one side, the house, garden and stable, while on the other side, the field at the foot of their mountain.

"What is it, Ulrich?" Sophie asked, sensing his struggle.

He looked at her for a moment. There was no right way to confess guilt. He took a deep breath. "Remember when I said that I had made mistakes in this place?"

"Uhum." Sophie waited.

"There was another person in our group, when we first woke up." He continued.

"That's why there were four horses." Sophie deducted.

"There was a woman, Sabrina." His eyes became distant, "She... looked a lot like you. I thought it was you." He struggled for words, "When I first woke up, I was still a little dazed from... Sophie, I chose to come here... to be with you."

Sophie looked at him but said nothing.

"I was very happy when I saw her... I hugged and kissed her." Ulrich paused. He looked for Sophie's reaction but she merely nodded.

"The instant I kissed her, I knew it was not you, but it was too late. Sabrina became obsessed with the idea that she was my twin. I did not... handle it well at all. She felt rejected." A shadow covered his eyes. "She left in the night. We found her body later."

Sophie took a deep breath. This man had just told her that a woman had died because of him. Yet, her son could have died because of her stupidity. She could not judge him. "What happened to Sabrina? I mean, I know what happened here but, what happened to her soul?" Sophie asked.

"I believe she would have to spend time in the ether then, probably go back to a third dimension world." Ulrich said quietly.

Sophie needed time to think, there was that other part to what he had said. Ulrich used the word 'twin' After Joshua's father left, she had met good men, who would have loved Josh. Three times she engaged, each time to a good man, and three times she broke the engagement. She had felt that none of the men had been good enough to be an example to her son. In addition, her heart sank when she though of spending the rest of her life with any of them. She made the decision to stay by herself until Josh was of age.

Sophie had learned about soul mates and twin souls through her research. She felt comfortable with the concept of soul mates because, sometimes, strangers felt like childhood friends, while others, gave her the willies. Twin flames was a different concept. For years, she had secretly wished for a dream relationship, like the one of the twin flames, without truly believing that it could happen to her. If Ulrich was her twin, that would explain all the memories and feelings of familiarity.

"You were with me, in the screen room, when she left." Sophie suddenly realized.

Ulrich looked at her, surprised. "Sophie, you had nothing to do with her... death."

"Ulrich, we have a problem. " Sophie said, staring at him.

"No... Sophie..." Ulrich said, almost agitated.

Sophie felt his apprehension. Her memories about Ulrich and how he came to be here, had been fragmented. The picture was becoming clearer. "I am indirectly responsible because I chose to come here. I was not meant to be here and you had waited for so long... They said that I had to choose between you and Josh... and I chose my son. I had given you up. Why did you follow me?"

Sophie stood up. She needed to breathe; to move away from him. *What has he done?* Her mind, frantic, searched through all the memories. It was bad enough that she had challenged the rules and chosen to follow her son; He had done even worse. He should not have cared. Souls in the seventh dimension are beyond fear, regret, loss and all the messy human emotions that we still carry into the fifth dimension. Something did not make sense. She turned to him and demanded, "Why did you follow me?"

His green eyes burned through her. "His soul is as precious to me, as it is to you."

At first, she did not understand, then, she remembered the night Josh was conceived. She could never forget that night. In the middle of lovemaking, she had looked up at Joshua's father and frozen. Under the light of the lamp she had seen a stranger. His eyes had been another's. It was as if his soul had left his body and another, taken residence. Sophie looked at Ulrich. "What are you truly saying?"

Ulrich's face was a stone mask. Carefully, he said. "It was me with you that night."

"Ulrich..." Sophie said in shock, still trying to sort through her thoughts. "I asked that the love I felt be true and long lasting. His father left but I got Josh."

"He is the personification of your love. He is a spark of the love you hold inside."

"How is that possible?"

"I am not sure Sophie... You did not ask for that man to love you. You asked for the emotion that you felt to be true and long lasting. The only way for the spark to be true, was for you to join with your twin." Ulrich said, almost thinking aloud.

Sophie sat down, in stunned silence. Ulrich, slowly, took a seat by her side. They were silent for a long time. Finally, Sophie said, "What a mess..."

Ulrich, carefully, put an arm around her and kissed her hair. "I love you... both."

Sophie slowly shook her head. "Ulrich, what are we going to do? There is no way to tell the repercussions of what we have done. One woman died and we are both to blame."

Ulrich thought for a moment. She was right, there was no way to imagine the ramifications. "All we can do is what we came here to do, Sophie; Look after the boy." he said.

Sophie stood and walked with her arms crossed for a while. Ulrich waited, sensing she was trying to decide their future. "Ulrich... other than the obvious, something else feels wrong. Is there anything else?" Sophie asked.

"Yes. There is still more you need to remember."

Sophie looked at him with apprehension.

"It is nothing like this." He reassured her. "It has to do with your abilities and why you came here, other than Josh, that is."

"Can you tell me?"

"I can but it won't make sense."

Now Sophie truly frowned. "I don't follow..." she shook her head.

"In this dimension, we get to exercise our imagination. The only limitations are within our own minds." Ulrich said.

"How come I don't entirely believe that?" She challenged.

"I don't know, Sophie. Perhaps, because you know that there are rules, such as, I can't tell you everything. I have to wait, and hope, that you remember and that, in itself, is a limitation."

Sophie remembered the concept of restriction. "Who made the rules? God loves... always gives."

"Good question. I don't truly know... It is knowledge that was communicated to me, like it usually is, in the ether." Ulrich had not considered the question.

"Who or what communicates the knowledge?" she asked.

Ulrich thought for a minute. "Generally, it is guides from the next level."

Sophie was trying to understand. She continued to search. "Can we communicate with fourth and third dimension humans?"

Ulrich felt puzzled at the question. The conversation was taking an unexpected twist. "Yes, it is a different type of communication."

"Can we travel back to those dimensions?" she asked.

He stood silent for a moment. He nodded then said: "You can..."

Sophie eyes burned through him. That was Ulrich's fear. Staring through him, she said: "You cannot have a physical presence, below the fifth, unless you borrow a body."

Ulrich paled at the question. "That is correct..."

Sophie was quiet for a while. She paced slowly with her arms crossed. Everything she had read, said that God loved humans. She didn't remember anything about God loving the ascended who, apparently, existed in some sort of bliss soup. An idea occurred to her. "Your dimension is beyond judgment, correct?"

"We do not judge." he confirmed.

"However, you feel love and longing." she added.

"We feel love but there is no more longing..." Ulrich corrected.

Looking deep into his eyes, she stated: "There is no more fear either... Correct?"

Ulrich hesitated at this question. "Correct..."

Sophie nodded in understanding. "How did you become aware that you were a drop of water in an ocean?"

Ulrich was visibly shaken. Sophie was approaching dangerous territory. "Through you..."

Sophie stared at him. Ulrich was not supposed to have felt longing, nor fear. Yet, to become an individual, our thoughts must be independent of the collective. Sophie began to feel anger. The word "oblivion" came to her, over and over... "These guides... the ones who communicate the rules... they are all waiting for their twin souls..."

Ulrich looked genuinely worried now. "Sophie..."

"Are they waiting for their twin souls to ascend, Ulrich?" Her eyes bore through him.

Ulrich sensed where she was going with this. "Yes."

Sophie tightened her jaw. "They really wanted us to ascend."

"That's what they do..." he said.

"Ulrich, what other reason did you have to come here?" She knew the answer but she wanted to hear it from him.

Ulrich stared at her hard. He took a deep breath and said, "I wanted to feel alive again. I saw you... back in old earth. I saw when you tuned into the energy of the planet... I saw how you, as a simple human, were able to see the world through the eyes of God. I felt alive through you and I was... afraid."

"You didn't want me to ascend." She finally understood.

"Sophie..." He looked genuinely worried. How could she forgive him.

"You became aware and afraid of oblivion."

Ulrich was at a loss for words.

"You borrowed a body and got me pregnant because you knew that I would never abandon that spark. It was an act of logic. At your level, there is no judgment, only logic. Your level pursues bliss and that's it." Sophie's eyes where sad.

"Sophie, I am truly..." He began to say.

"Sorry? Ulrich, think about it. What did you want?"

Ulrich briefly glanced away, then back at her. "To feel alive and to be with you... I wanted to feel alive with you."

"You are alive and, by the looks of it, full of emotion. You did not feel guilt, until you became physical in the fifth dimension." she said evenly.

Ulrich was besides himself. He had felt apprehension at the prospect of loosing the awareness of her.

"Are you truly my twin?" she asked.

Sophie could feel his struggle but it was his eyes that told the story. "Yes." he said.

Sophie came to Ulrich and caressed his face. Ulrich's green eyes burned through her. He grabbed her hand and held it tight. Tentatively, he stepped closer to her. Sophie stood fast. Ulrich's other hand came up her waist to her back and gently pulled her to him.

They stood, pressed against each other and looked into each other's eyes, until they lost sense of their surroundings. Sophie felt herself become lighter. He felt her heart pound against his chest. They knew each other. Sophie loved the feel of his body against her, his scent...

Ulrich lowered his head and touched her lips with his own. He remembered the fullness and softness of her lips. She wrapped her arms around him and held him tightly. Their bodies felt energized and buoyant at the same time. Life pulsated through them and from them. They closed their eyes and their minds became fluid. They could not tell where one ended and the other began. He kissed her for a very long time, gently, deeply.

After a while, Sophie rested her head on his chest and whispered, "I really don't believe that God made those rules..."

Ulrich pressed her harder to him. He ran his fingers through her hair, caressed the back of her neck then, gently massaged her back. "Sophie, will you forgive me?" He didn't truly regret what he did because his action had guaranteed his expulsion from the seventh dimension but it had been wrong to trick her.

"Josh is a gift, Ulrich." she said. "The question is, will you forgive yourself."

"I... am at odds..." Ulrich had not understood the implications.

"Ulrich, how many other beings from your level fathered children with their twins?" She was trying to get him to see a portion of the truth.

Ulrich tightened his hold on Sophie. He remembered the days before he left and was stunned beyond words. He saw legions. "Before me, none... after me, many..."

Still resting her head on his chest, she said, almost whispering: "Uhum. When you sit in those levels, everything is very fluid. Like water, a drop of ink, eventually, changes the color of all the water in a glass. Those around you, became aware of oblivion... through you... they felt life through you. When you left, they missed you. They became aware of the difference, then they became aware of themselves again... and rebelled."

Ulrich held her for a long time. He did not want to let her go. Inside his mind there were so many confused thoughts. How could he had been so... there were no words to describe... selfish, stupid, short-sighted. Even Sophie, now, did not realize the magnitude of what he had done. He had wanted to experience life with her. He did not want to loose her to bliss. In bliss, there would have been no "him" and "her", just "we"... and that "we" included billions of souls.

Ulrich had waited for so long to join to his twin. At one time there was nothing he had wanted more than bliss. He grew impatient. He watched as she went through life, searching. He felt drawn to her. Sophie met a walk-in who had agreed to let Ulrich inhabit him for a short while.

Later, he saw with sadness, when the walk-in suggested that she end the pregnancy... the walk-in did not feel attachment to the child. Sophie considered the option but her soul screamed. Ulrich stayed by her side, as she raised Josh alone. He communicated with her through dreams, whispers and urgings of her heart. He loved them and loved seeing the world through their eyes.

The energies became unstable on earth and the elders decided to allow awakened souls to transition. Other dimension beings did not want to give up the earth, so they did all they could to delay the cycle. Meantime, the bodies of the transitioned souls were kept in stasis. Earth had changed... all the dynamics had changed. It was a big mess. Ulrich watched and waited, back in his dimension.

He never stopped to think about the impact he had on those souls around him. Millions of souls exist in a point and even more at the angles. Ulrich realized now that it would have been impossible not to have an impact. Ascended souls live in bliss, anything else is immediately detected. It is like the transition from warm water to cold.

Humans have a simple concept of heaven as three dimensional. In reality, there are infinite dimensions and infinite levels. Sophie was right, it was impossible to imagine the ramifications. His thoughts now, were with the souls who rebelled and the children they fathered. *They could have landed anywhere...* If they had been separated from their twins, they would feel lost and confused. They were in danger of experiencing abandonment, which is the door to pain, fear and anger. Angry souls are bad news in any dimension.

Ulrich hugged her even harder. Something in his chest constricted into itself and he felt pain. Finally, he said in a hoarse whisper, "Sophie... I have to go away... for a while."

"What?" Sophie froze. She had been resting her head on his chest and enjoying the warmth. She had felt his struggle, vaguely, so the statement took her a little by surprise. Sophie took a deep breath. "Why?" she asked.

Ulrich's face denoted struggle. "I have to know what happened to those souls... and their children." he said.

"Ok, I think I see why." She finally said. The look in his eyes made her smile. "Ulrich, it's going to be Ok. Until recently, I did not believe that twin souls existed. The soul is eternal, remember? I know now, that you are always with me." she said calmly then, with a glint in her eyes, she added, "It would have been nice to snuggle up to you at night, though..."

Ulrich shook his head and smiling, bent down to kiss her again. Still holding her, he promised to come back as soon as he could.

"Yeah, Ok... now come tell the others, otherwise I will never hear the end of it." she said, with mock annoyance.

They walked back to the house and Ulrick called their names, one by one. He asked them to join him in the main hall. Iksha was the first to appear.

"Hello dears." She greeted them sweetly. She had been in her garden, tending to her babies, when she heard Ulrich in her mind.

One by one, the others joined them in the main hall. Josh came to sit by his mother. "Are you Ok?" He asked her. He could sense that something was wrong.

Sophie smiled and squeezed his hand. "I'm Ok."

"I have to go away for a while." Ulrich said simply. He told them that he needed to travel to find out what happened to a group of beings from another dimension. "I don't know how long it will take to get the information that I need." he said.

"We just arrived here. Why do you have to leave now. You didn't say anything about this before..." Edgardo asked.

"What beings are these, dear?" Iksha asked. She perceived a complication.

"Souls from the seventh dimension." Ulrich said, without disclosing much. He did not feel comfortable sharing with them intimate details about his relationship with Sophie.

Tamara and Iksha looked at Sophie. Neither woman could tune into either Sophie nor Ulrich. *Complete blackout...* Tamara thought. *There is something big going on and these two are like stones...*

Sophie stood up and faced the group. "We will continue to prepare for the arrival of the newcomers. Josh, what can you tell us?" she asked, turning to her son. He had been practicing remote viewing.

"Uhum. There is about two groups approaching this area. They are families with, mostly, teenagers." Josh said.

"You can see them in detail... that means that they must be close." Sophie reasoned aloud.

Tamara wanted to know how pressing was Ulrich's business, so she asked, "Couldn't you stay until the newcomers are settled in?"

"Ulrich does not have to stay. He has something to take care of... My Mom and myself were building and preparing this place before you guys got here... Granted, you have made things much more easier but we can handle it." Josh interjected.

Ulrich nodded. "It is important that I find if any of those souls incarnated here. They may need help." He explained, to satisfy Tamara's curiosity. He could tell them that other souls needed help and they would understand that. He did not want to tell them that, if any of those souls ran into the wrong group of people, they could become a problem.

"Will you stay for dinner, dear?" Iksha asked. There was no point in trying to get information from, either Ulrich or Sophie, at this time. Iksha felt that, in time, they would learn the details.

"Certainly." Ulrich answered warmly.

Tamara watched Sophie and Ulrich all through dinner. She could tell, by their body language, that they had become much more than friends. *These two have a heavy secret...* She would have to wait until Ulrich was gone to get a moment with Sophie. Maybe she would able to read her then.

Ulrich had avoided additional questions by focusing the conversation on work that needed to be done around the castle. He explained to Edgardo and Josh how to build the smoker that Iksha had requested. Sophie agreed to manifest the meats and other food stuff, while Chul-Moo would provide the tools and utensils.

They finished dinner in silence. Iksha, Edgardo, Tamara and Chul-Moo wished Ulrich a safe trip and prompt return. Iksha understood that Ulrich wanted to have a word with Sophie and Josh, so she herded the others out of the room. Ulrich turned to Josh and Sophie. "I know that you will look after each other and the others. Sophie, I noticed that you blocked Tamara's probes, does Josh know how to do that?"

"I do." Josh said.

They both turned to him. "Oh... what else do you know?" Sophie asked her son, with a raised eyebrow.

"Well... I can read body language and it is pretty obvious that something is worrying you two..." he said evenly.

Ulrich nodded. He turned to Sophie and, holding her by the elbow, guided her to the front entrance. He turned to Josh and motioned for him to follow.

Once outside, Josh gave them a knowing look. "Seven dimension beings needing help? Really? If the others didn't see through that... You are seven D, right? You can take care of yourself, and then some... I believe you're going to check on your kind but not because they need help. Unless... there is something bigger after them..."

Sophie blinked twice. It was true, an aware seven D would not have anything to fear in this dimension. "Would these souls be aware, Ulrich?"

"That's what I'm going to find out." he said, still looking at Josh. "Sophie... I have to leave now." He bend down and gave her a light kiss. In his mind, he asked Josh to stay.

"Are you coming sweetie?" Sophie asked Josh.

"No, I want to have a word with Ulrich, Mom. I'll drop by to say goodnight.

Sophie looked from Josh to Ulrich. She did not like being left out of the conversation. Her son looked older and more mature. *He should have a moment with his father,* she thought to herself. She hugged him, gave one last smile to Ulrich then, turned away.

In silence, they smiled and watched as the Termite scrambled to stay close to her mistress. Once the door had closed behind them, Josh turned to Ulrich and waited. Ulrich regarded his son for a moment, torn between telling him the truth or not. He decided that it was better to leave that for later.

"Josh, you are very perceptive… and gifted. There are scouts around the area. Please be careful and look after your Mom."

"I will look after Mom but honestly… " Josh began to say that he would feel sorry for anyone who messed with his Mom, when Ulrich interrupted him.

"That's exactly what worries me. I know that your Mother can take care of herself. It is you who needs to be careful. Don't take unnecessary risks. Don't go out looking for marauders. Josh… she should not get angry. It would not be a good thing if she gets angry."

Josh was about to express a smart remark, when the look in Ulrich's eyes stopped him. This man was actually worried. "What could happen?" he asked, frowning.

"I don't know... I just know that she can visualize, just about, anything and make it happen." Ulrich said. "Josh, I will try to contact you or your Mom but I am not sure if I will be able..."

Josh nodded. "Any idea how long will it take you..." he asked. Josh had the strong feeling that this trip would not be easy for Ulrich.

Ulrich nodded. The boy was perceptive. "Time is different where I am going. I just want to get information about the beings that landed here. Stay close to your Mom or, at least, in mind contact at all times. I will come back." he finally said.

Josh watched as Ulrich sat in Sukhasana and closed his eyes. Slowly, he became translucent then, he was no longer there. Josh blinked twice. He felt something like sadness but shook if off. *I'm tired. It's been a long day...* "Let's go boy." he petted Bear, who never left his side, and went back into the castle.

13

FLYING HORSES

Sometimes, she wondered if she was dreaming. There they were, master builders, having hardly used any tools. *It is a castle now...* Sophie thought, as she walked into the main hall. She bumped into Edgardo who had been working on a relief. Every time she turned around, it seemed, there was a new detail on the walls.

"Pretty soon, there won't be walls left for you to decorate, Edgardo." she joked.

"Esta bien... there is still the cave and, after that, I'll just work on the stones outside." he said, grinning.

In less than a week, everything had changed. To keep her mind occupied, Sophie became driven. At first her energy drove the others and they worked around the clock. That type of drive cannot be sustained by food alone, so Sophie taught the others how to tap into their minds. Work really took off when the others also learned to draw energy from the environment.

Iksha became an expert on food preservation. She accumulated stores of meat, cheese and grains. Josh fashioned a smoker for her, which she kept hot around the clock. At Edgardo's prodding, she finally relented and encouraged grapes to grow. Rows of wine barrels slumbered into maturity in the cellar.

Tamara became an artist with thread. Chul-Moo created metallic strands for her, which she used to weave light into her fabrics. Soon after, everybody in the household wore bright colors with glimmery details. Even the castle walls and furnishings bore the stamp of her work.

Josh experimented with the vibration of matter until he was able to contain and store the energy of chemical reactions. He created stones that absorbed daylight and released the stored energy at night. He placed his stones all over inside the castle and in the cave. Finally, he created a fire that never goes out for Chul-Moo's forge.

Sophie assisted and encouraged everyone. She also developed methods for manifesting glass, paper and ink. She studied nature and learned to communicate with the animals of the forest. Sophie learned to discern different energies and to tune into animals to see the world through their eyes. She developed new abilities, such as, reconstituting organic matter and dispersing the molecules of damaging micro-organisms.

Every one thought about Ulrich but they avoided mention of his name in consideration to Sophie. Her attitude had made it clear that she preferred to focus on creation. It was true. As soon as she had a chance, Tamara tried to pry. It was useless. Sophie changed the conversation and when Tamara insisted, she felt Sophie's annoyance. Sophie's energy was like a blow. Tamara felt drained and recoiled.

"Look, I am sorry, Tamara but when I say that I don't want to talk about something..." Sophie began to tell the girl, contrite.

"That's OK girl... I get you...." Tamara interrupted. She was not sure what it was that she had felt but she decided that it was better to get off the subject. "Listen, I have a new shade of red that will look good with your hair. Let's go make a dress for you."

Sophie took a deep breath. She knew Tamara would try again, it was her nature. However, it was better to focus on something positive. If two people insist on seeing an argument to it's end, they actually loose more than they gain. "I'd love that. Thank you." she said.

Back at the stables, Josh and Chul-Moo measured the horses for shoes. Josh petted the stallion. He spoke softly but with confidence. "Eins, let me see that foot... Now that you guys sleep in the stable, your nails may become brittle. We need to make you some shoes..."

Horses hoofs stay healthy, in the wild, thanks to slow wear and dry conditions. The stables would protect them in winter but, in the summer, it might be too moist. In addition, now the horses carried them through mountainous terrain. The guys had decided that the horses needed to have their hoofs protected.

He had just finished with Eins and was about to work on Zwei, when he had a vision. He saw the newcomers clearly. They were running towards the fields at the bottom of the mountains. A group of marauders pursued them. Josh didn't wait to see any more and called Sophie, in his mind.

Sophie's head shot up and she raised a hand to Tamara. "There's trouble." she said, and immediately ran to find Josh. She met him running from the stables.

"Mom, the newcomers are being chased by marauders." Josh said.

"Where?" Sophie asked, then remembered that she could tune into the creatures. "They're down by the river." she said, without waiting for Joshua's answer.

"We need to help them." Josh already had the horses with them. He jumped on Eins and turned to face his Mom. "Well?"

Sophie had no idea what they were going to do but she agreed. She lifted herself on Zwei and directed her to the path.

"We're not going to make it Mom. Take us there." Josh called after her.

"What?" Sophie did not understand what Josh wanted.

"You lifted stones heavier than the horses... TAKE US THERE!" He called again.

Sophie understood. She visualized the meadow and made sure that there were no life signs. Ulrich's words came back to her... *Make sure that your landing is clear.* She then, lifted herself, the horses and Josh in the direction of the meadow. The horses, surprised, continued their running motion, which made them look as if they were galloping on air.

Below, by the river, two groups of newcomers had converged, one chased by marauders. The newcomers had followed the dreams and hoped to meet Sophie and her son soon. They had not expected to have to defend themselves. It had not occurred to them to make weapons.

Neither the newcomers nor marauders were prepared for what they saw next. Two huge black horses, came galloping from the sky. The riders, a man and a woman, looked impressive. The woman, barefoot, had long black hair and wore a flowing red dress. The man wore sandals and had a leather apron, over buff pants and white shirt. It was a striking apparition but not the image of warriors.

The marauders stopped cold, while the newcomers continued to run. Sophie had spoken into their minds and reassured them. *We are here to protect you. Get behind us.* She had told them. To herself, Sophie figured that she could lift the marauders and drop them far from there.

The horses landed with heavy thumps and came to a halt not too far from the marauders. The animals looked fierce; black, huge, excitedly pawning at the ground, their muscles rippled all over. Sophie surveyed the group of marauders. They were a group of about twenty burly men. While Sophie surveyed the men, Josh began to vibrate the stones in the area.

The marauders stood in shock for a minute then, one of them asked, "Who are you?"

"We live on the mountains. Leave these people alone." Sophie answered.

One of the marauders turned to his companions and told them that it was trick. "They have nothing!" he yelled. "It is just a woman and a boy!" he smirked.

Sophie felt her anger raise but, before she had a chance to react, Josh gathered the stones into a ribbon of molten rock. The heated stones had become swirling lava. Intense heat and light emanated from the shape. Josh raised the ribbon high, so that all could see. Lava flowed up from the ground in coils. Josh shaped the lava into a giant snake and the man and his companions stood transfixed.

"What are you?" one of the marauders asked.

"We are peaceful but we can defend ourselves. We will defend ourselves and our people" she told the marauder's. Sophie knew that this was not the time for details. Apparently, neither did Josh because he made the snake spit. Blobs of lava flew through the air and landed in front of the marauders like fiery cannon balls. Flames and dirt burst from the impacts, creating chaos among their group.

Most of the marauders did not wait for another attack. Almost all the men, at the same time, turned and ran away. Two of the men stared at Sophie and Josh for a moment, then turned and also left. Josh waited until he felt that the marauders were far then, he allowed the stones cool. Lava solidified into stone and, there it stood, a thirty foot stone snake raising from its coils. In time, people would marvel at the skill of the artist who had carved that image.

Self conscious, Sophie turned to the newcomers. "Hello... we are glad that you are here..."

The newcomers were three families with teenagers. A tiny redhead was the first to speak. "What the hell was that... fire thing? I heard a voice in my mind... Was that you?" .

Sophie liked her instantly. The woman was as short as Iksha and just as full of energy. For a moment she amused herself, wondering how those two would get along, then quickly answered. "It is not safe here. We should go to the castle. There you can eat, rest and then we can talk more." Sophie told them, avoiding details.

"Castle?" one of the teenagers raised an eyebrow.

Josh motioned for him to turn around and look up. Up on the shelf, stood the castle overshadowed by the mountains behind.

"Neat, what is the name of that place?" the kid asked.

Sophie and Josh exchanged blank looks. It had not occurred to them to think of a name.

Josh was the first to speak. "Schloss Am See?" he offered.

"Castle by The Lake?" Ok, I'll go with that, Sophie said. She turned to the teenager and the people. "It is Schloss Am See." Sophie clicked her tongue and turned Zwei towards the mountains. "You're using German words now..." Sophie commented to Josh. She wondered if Josh had heard from Ulrich.

"Oh, yeah... You know I loved German in school and Ulrich was helping me practice... before he left." Josh said then, began to ask her about him. "Have you..."

"No..." she shook her head. She was about to tell him that she would try to contact him with intention, when the curious stares around them, brought her back to the present. "Ulrich is another one of us. He is traveling now." She offered as explanation.

Josh dismounted and loaned his ride to the little redhead and her daughter. He turned to the newcomers and introduced himself. "Hi, I'm Josh and this is my Mom, Sophie." then he motioned for them to follow him. "This way..." and he proceeded to move in the direction of the path.

Sophie remained on her horse because she was barefoot and because she preferred the vantage point. Josh walked ahead with Eins, while Sophie brought up the rear. "Stay close to each other please. Josh will tell you the story of when we woke up on this meadow. Listen to him." Sophie called out to the group and trotted away from one of the ladies who had tried to engage her in conversation. She did not like to be out on the open with a group of defenseless people and small talk was a distraction.

There were four adult males, four adult females, seven teenagers and one mature woman. They looked tired and dirty. Sophie noticed the mature woman. She was a tall blonde, probably in her early sixties. Sophie asked her if she was Ok.

"Well honey... I could use some iced tea. No, make that a shower, clean clothes, food and then, some iced tea." the lady said with a tired smile.

Sophie leaned forward and offered her hand to the lady. With an amused look, the lady took it and Sophie swiftly lifted her to her horse. "That should help a little. Hang on, Ok?" she said.

"Child... how did you do that? You're no bigger than a minute! " the lady said, surprised at Sophie's strength.

Sophie so loved to hear the lady's accent. She had retired from the military and stayed to live in the south. At first, she did not like it. Eventually, she figured the heat might have something to do with the slow and roundabout way people approached situations. She gave up on trying to understand them and decided to just enjoy them. Instead of giving her a direct answer, Sophie asked, "Have you heard about the power of intention?"

The lady thought for a minute then, smiled. "You mean to create things with our thoughts? Yes, I have..."

Sophie nodded. "That's how." she said. Sophie liked this lady. She exuded warmth. Sophie had the feeling that it would not take long for this lady to grasp the principles of intention. The rode in silence with Sophie scanning the horizon, alert.

"You feel they're watching us?" the lady asked.

"Yes. I don't think all of them ran away. I still feel some of their energy." Sophie said, not surprised at the woman's intuition. She bend forward and whispered to her mare. "Zwei, we could use more of your friends."

As they approached the site of their first camp, Sophie was not surprised to see a small group of horses. Josh turned to her with a knowing smile. Instead of waiting, the horses calmly came to meet them. At first, the group of newcomers were shy about the animals but the gentle giants won them over. Among comments about their size and beauty, the newcomers managed to select a horse. Josh and Sophie transferred their passengers to new mounts and soon, the group resumed their journey up the mountains.

Sophie felt more relaxed, now that the newcomers had mounts. She felt that if the marauders tried anything, the horses would take the newcomers to safety. She maintained her attention focused on the surrounding areas, however, she did allow a bit of herself to enjoy the trip and getting to know the newcomers.

Right after they passed the lake, they ran into Edgardo, trailed by two very vocal dogs. "We saw everything! We were worried about you until we saw that magnificent fire snake... it was you, Josh. Verdad?" the man beamed with excitement.

Sophie and Josh had left in a hurry and barely given any instructions to Chul-Moo. Edgardo and Chul-Moo had been about to ride, when Iksha screamed at them to stop. Tamara and Iksha had stood near the edge of the shelf and watched as red hot stones clumped together to form the snake. All four had witnessed the whole episode.

"Err... yes." Josh nodded, more than self conscious. He had avoided questions about the snake, until that moment.

The newcomers were shocked. Most of them, had assumed that the snake and the horses had been sent by a higher power. They looked at Josh and Sophie with apprehension. Sophie shook her head and began to explain. "We are in a place where you can create things with your mind. We come from earth. To judge by your language and expressions, so do you. Josh has been able to tell you about the first two days, when we woke up on the meadow. We didn't become aware of our abilities until later..."

"How long have you been here?" Jacob, one of the teenagers interrupted.

Sophie and Josh looked at each other. Surprised, they realized that they had been there less than fifteen days. "Yes, and we build the castle in less than three days!" Edgardo said, clearly proud of their achievements.

"Three days? Is that thing safe?" Chloe, a cute dishwater blonde with intelligent eyes, said with raised eyebrows.

"Of course it is. We live there." Edgardo answered, clearly offended. "My work is good."

Sophie repressed a smile and said, "Edgardo is our master stone mason. He is very good at what he does."

"What else do we have?" the mature lady asked, approaching her horse to Sophie's.

"We have master gardener, weaver and a... metallurgist." Sophie answered.

They arrived at the shelf and the conversation turned to the castle. Iksha and Tamara were at the front entrance. Iksha, as expected, was generous with her hugs and greetings. Tamara was also friendly but much less effusive. She took mental note of the number of people and their body types. Weaving provided her with deep satisfaction and she welcomed new models for her creations.

Sophie allowed them a few moments to acquaint themselves with the residents and the animals then, she asked Edgardo if he would show the newcomers to the bedrooms. Finally, she turned to the lady and asked her if she would prefer a main level room.

"Call me Nan and, yes, I don't like stairs."

Sophie turned to Iksha. Before she could ask the question, Iksha came forward and took Nan by the arm. "Come with me, dear. There is a room, not too far from mine, that I think you will love."

Chul-Moo took Zwei's reins then, pointed to the new horses. "What do you want me to do about the rest?" he asked Sophie.

She turned to the horses. "Would you like to stay with us or will you prefer to go back to the meadow?" In her mind, she saw the meadow and the horses galloping happy and free. Then she saw the land covered in snow and the horses by the castle. "Oh... I get it. You guys want your summer vacation, then you will be back by winter. Ok, I think we can have stables ready for you by then." she said smiling. Sophie turned to Chul-Moo and said, "Let them go."

It was late afternoon by the time the newcomers had washed and put on clean clothes. Tamara had accumulated a collection of pieces that, after minor adjustments, fitted each of them. Wishing to avoid delays, Sophie had distributed the clothes with the intention that each would find the right wearer.

They trickled downstairs, where Sophie waited for them. Iksha, Tamara and Sophie had prepared one of the tables in the main hall. Iksha proudly displayed a collection of dishes worthy of a banquet. The newcomers ate until satisfied. It had been days since they had a proper meal. The ladies appreciated being able to sit at a table, instead of having to clean the catch of the day. After dinner, they appreciated Iksha's sweet berry tarts and aromatic tea.

Fresh from a three dimensional world, the newcomers wondered if they had died and if this was heaven. Sophie smiled and reassured that they were alive and it was not heaven. "This is the fifth dimension..." she began to say.

"Excuse me... did you say that we are in a different dimension? That is impossible." one of the men interjected.

"What do you think this is then?" asked Sophie.

"I don't know... a bad dream?" the man answered back.

Sophie nodded. "I can see why anyone would think that. The question is... what difference would it make?"

"A dream is not real and we get to wake up." he man retorted.

Sophie nodded again. "Do you wish to stake your life on that belief?"

"What do you mean?" the man said, frowning.

"If it is a dream... why did you run from the marauders?"

"Because... I was not armed... I have my family..." he said, as if stating the obvious.

"Exactly. Regardless of the nature of this reality. The fact is that we are here. You can choose to listen to us , who have been here a little longer. Allow us to share with you what we have learned... or you can choose to take your family with you and go live your dream elsewhere." Sophie said evenly, however, her stare burned through the man. Sophie felt tired and impatient.

Silence froze the hall. It was not so much what Sophie said but the energy behind her delivery. Her annoyance hit them like a sound wave. The man nodded, silent.

"Very well then... This, is post-apocalyptic earth; I do not know how many hundred or even thousands of years after the cataclysms. We were taken from old earth and preserved in safety, until the earth healed. The energy of the planet is such that our thoughts can become real. There are individual limitations. In time, we will go over these limitations.

The people who attacked you are called the marauders. They are descendants from the original survivors. It seems that not everyone on earth was rescued. I remember some of the literature of the time. I read that a person had to be, at least, fifty one percent service to others, in order to be rescued. We could say that service to others people prefer cooperation instead of dominance.

Later, tomorrow, I would like you think of the activities that brought you joy, back in old earth. What consistently gave you joy over the years, is an important clue. We could say that our gifts emerge from what gives us joy."

The newcomers felt their brains stretched to capacity. They had so many questions. What happened to earth? What was this fifth dimension? Who had rescued them? Gifts? What kind of gifts?

Sophie tried to answer their questions without going into too many details. Continued conversation would only take away time that they could use to replenish their energies. It was getting late, so Sophie concluded. "It is late. I will stop now. It has been a trying day... It will take time to absorb everything."

The newcomers sat, for a while, commenting to each other. Finally, one of the men asked, "How long can we stay here?"

"You can stay here as long as you wish. This place has been prepared for you." Sophie said.

Another man raised his hand. "What about the marauders. Is this all of you? We should set guards..." he said. Until the change, he had been a soldier.

Sophie nodded. "I can understand your concern. In time, we may have to resort to that. Tonight, however, I can tell you that the marauders will not come here." she said and secretly wished he did not ask for further explanations. She knew that they were tired and needed to rest. Night watch would be an unnecessary waste of energy.

The man insisted. "How can you guarantee that they won't come here?" Sophie sighed. She wished she could just transfer her knowledge to them. She remembered how patient Ulrich had been with them and wondered if she would ever be as good as he had been. "I keep watch on the mountain." she finally said.

"How?" the man insisted.

Josh stood up. "How do you think we knew that you needed our help? I saw you in my mind. Have you forgotten what you saw? My Mom communicates with the creatures of the forest. They are nocturnal. Should anything disturb them, they will wake up my Mom."

"My awareness is always divided." Sophie added. "I am here with you and also receiving impressions from the forest." Sophie smiled tired. She stood up and went to the kitchen. Iksha and Tamara followed.

Still not able to understand, the man decided to keep watch himself. He recruited two other men to help him. People fresh from the third dimension, carry their beliefs with them. Back in the kitchen, Iksha handed Sophie a cup of mint tea. Sophie accepted it, a little absentminded, and looked around the kitchen. She loved this kitchen.

It was the summer so only the grill remained hot. Every morning, Josh lighted a small fire in all the hearths in the house. The fires burned for about two hours, then he allowed them to die out. It was just enough to chase the early morning chill off the stone walls. The tea was sweet and hot. She closed her eyes and thought about the day they found the honey bees.

"You don't like questions much, do you?" Tamara poked. She felt confident that Sophie would not loose her temper with Iksha around.

Iksha turned to Tamara. "You need to learn when to stop, Tamara. If you had to spend half the energy that Sophie spends every day, perhaps you would understand." she scolded.

"I'm just playing... She is always so serious." Tamara answered.

She had a point. It seemed that, after Ulrich left, Sophie had forgotten how to laugh. She had taken upon herself the responsibility of everyone's safety. She could have asked for assistance but she had wanted to be busy. She got her wish.

"It's true... I don't have much patience and... it gets worse when I'm tired. I'm going to bed now." she hugged Iksha and Tamara then left.

On her way upstairs, she stopped by Josh and the group of teenagers. She ruffled her son's hair and told him to stay inside the castle that night. "I would like to get some sleep and if you, or any of you guys, go wandering about, the animals will wake me up. I'll let the animals know about the night watch."

Josh smiled. "Good night, Mom."

Joshua and the teenagers had chosen to sit aside. Young people have their own set of questions and concerns. The dogs had given them the opportunity to establish conversation about something other than themselves.

"What type of dogs are these?" Chloe asked, petting Bear.

"Well, Bear is a mix of rottweiler and lab." Josh said, pointing to the big, black dog. "...and that is the Termite, although, back in the old world, sometimes we called her pestilence because if she kissed you that was it... you got a sore throat. That dog will eat, just about, anything."

"C'mere pesticide..." one of the boys called to the scruffy gray dog.

Josh and the other kids laughed good naturedly. "No... pestilence..." they corrected the boy.

They talked about their previous lives; the pets and friends they had left behind. Many had been gamers so they found several common bonds. Finally, they exchanged impressions about waking up in a different world.

Eventually, the adult newcomers accepted that they were exhausted and, reluctantly, said their good nights. Only Chul-Moo, the ex-soldier and a couple of the men stayed. Chul-Moo declared "We must make weapons. These marauders have come too close. We must arm our people." He explained what he did. The ex-soldier and the men said they wanted to learn. They decided to meet sometime so that Chul-Moo could take them to the forge.

14

THEY FLY, SING AND
THE STONE SNAKE SMILES

That night, Sophie thought of Ulrich. She had not heard from him and wondered if she would ever hear from him again. She laid on her bed and thought of all that had transpired between them. A part of her wished that he had never followed her.

Back in old earth, she had resigned herself to solitude. Ulrich had shattered her peace. Part of her resented him and part of her missed him. *I hate these spiritual lessons.* Finally, she drifted into sleep.

During the day time hours, Sophie did not have time to worry about Ulrich anymore. The newcomers became the castle residents. There were chores, lessons and surveillance. Her attention was stretched, almost to it's limits. She kept in constant communion with the creatures of the forest and even the meadow. She also kept in constant attention to know where each one of the castle residents were. They asked her question after question. Sometimes she wished there were more copies of her.

The adults turned to be more trouble than the teenagers. They had lived longer in a world where words were expressed carelessly. They were good people who had been too busy providing for their families, to stop to think about the messages of fear that had been disseminated in that world. Instead of encouraging, they had learned to scold. Instead of dreaming, they had learned to be realistic, *whatever that meant.*

In addition, they wanted to fit what had happened, to their idea of an apocalypse. Instead of moving forward, they lingered for hours discussing theories about the nature of the cataclysms, what type of people had survived and what countries. They tried to find blame. Sometimes, Sophie truly wearied of their chat. Under different circumstances, she would have welcomed debate. These days her attention was much too stretched for such a luxury.

The only one, who did not pressure her, was Nan. The lady's warmth helped her feel at ease. Sophie loved to spend time with Nan. Other than Iksha, Nan was one of the few people with whom Sophie chatted about her past.

One day, Sophie told Nan a story about her and Josh, when he was a five year old. While in college, Sophie had lived with her son in a tiny house by the woods. She realized that they had a mouse problem when, cleaning a closet, a mouse came out running. Josh had been helping her but he had not seen the mouse.

Instead of running away, the critter ran to Sophie. The mouse actually ran over her foot. Sophie freaked. She yelled at the thing: "Get off me you asshole!" while she shook her foot. The little guy flew through the air and, when it landed, Thomas, their Tabby, caught it and ran out the room with it. Sophie chased after Thomas. Josh chased after Sophie and, Dutch, their big German Shepherd, chased after them all.

Thomas paused by the front door. Sophie slammed into the wall but immediately opened the door. Out Thomas went, with his catch. Sophie felt a split second of relief then, Dutch barreled through the open door. Sophie and Josh ran outside in chase of Dutch. It took them a while to get the dog to stop and come back with them. Sophie was too shaken to worry about the cat and Josh looked like he was going to bust a seam laughing. "Mom... you called the mouse an asshole..." he had said, in delighted shock at his mother using a bad word.

Nan laughed with such mirth that she levitated. Then she truly began to laugh. That was the breakthrough that she had needed. It became easier for Nan to explore her emotions and tune into mirth. She discovered her gifts through laughter.

In turn, Nan was able to teach the other inhabitants. That lifted an enormous load off Sophie. Once they saw how one of them, could do things that they had believed impossible, they began to believe in the possibility of the impossible. Released from societies' constraints, eventually, one by one, began to share in their childhood memories. They remembered children stories and movies. They talked about the dreams of their youth. Sophie was finally able to relax a little more.

The teenagers were much easier. It is natural for a young person to exercise her imagination. They first began to talk about how much fun it would be to fly. They allowed themselves to dream aloud and they levitated.

There were a couple of mishaps, such as when Nick, a smart alecky, chatty boy managed to fly himself into a tree. Nick had all the willingness to learn but none of the discipline required to do so safely. Sophie had to put a restriction on him. Nick challenged Sophie's authority, when she recommended that he did not fly for a while.

"You are not my mother." he had retorted.

Sophie looked at him, amused. She turned to his mother and asked if she could put him in "time out" Nick's mother said yes and wished her luck.

"Oh, he will listen..." Sophie said.

Nick gave her a defiant look which Sophie ignored. She said, "SIT." and with the power of her mind, sat him on the chair behind him. The force was impossible to describe. There was no standing against it. Nick sat yelling at her to release him.

Sophie calmly said, "Silence." and, even though his mouth moved, no sound came out of it.

Nicks parent's stifled a smile. Part of them enjoyed the fact that Nick had met with authority, nevertheless, they asked if Nick would be OK. What if he needed help?

"Disparaging remarks will be soundless. Only when he is open to conversation, will he be heard." Sophie said. She then turned to Nick. "You will stay here and watch Tamara work. Pay attention to how she focuses on the weave. Learn."

In order to get him to focus, Sophie made him work with Tamara. He had to learn weaving. He could not leave, nor aggravate them with words. Begrudgingly, he resigned himself to learn.

There was no carefree way to make fabric. When he did not focus, the fabric came out looking like a cat had trained its claws on it. He could not hide his mental disposition. Finally, he learned to focus until his fabric came out smooth and beautiful. He did not love to weave but he loved the feeling of accomplishment. He could call Sophie now and show her that he could focus.

Sophie smiled, satisfied, at the results. "Ok... now let's think about what it takes to fly." Sophie released him from his chair and took him to the kitchen. There, she offered a snack and sat down to talk with him. Nick felt better about himself now. He did not like that Sophie had disciplined him but realized that she could have done worse things to him.

They talked about the place where his mind needed to be. How much attention could he dedicate to flying, if for example, a bird crossed his path. Would he look at the bird and fly himself into the mountain or would he be able to appreciate the beauty of animal's contortions, without forgetting about his own direction?

They talked about his strength. What would it feel like, after being up in the air for spans of time. Sophie said, "Well Nick, let's see how long it takes you get tired."

Outside, Nick found that, after one hour, he felt tired. Sophie talked to him about drawing energy from the environment. He was able to do so at a small rate. Nick had been small and wiry to begin with, a sign that either he was too hyper or did not care about food. They agreed that he should always time his flights so that he would not deplete his energy.

"At least, carry sunflower seeds and water with you always." Sophie told him.

Then, there was Chloe. She had always loved to sing and now she was able to modulate her voice and even make different sounds with her vocal chords. Then she moved to getting the birds to sing with her. She practiced for hours until she practically had hundred of birds chirping different tones at different intervals. It was a veritable symphony.

The downside was that the birds invaded Iksha's garden. Sophie stood with crossed arms and one fist against her mouth, to keep from laughing. Iksha did not think that it was a laughing matter.

"I can't get in to tend to my babies. Everywhere I look, there is a bird. I don't want to step on them!"

Sophie managed to work an agreement. "Iksha, the birds love berries. How about we create another patch, just for them? That way they can be fed and Chloe can keep her friends around?"

Iksha agreed, which in turn opened an avenue for another one of the teenagers to discover an ability.

A boy named Brandon loved to do the wave with his arms. That was his standard greeting. He even waved both arms unconsciously. Brandon was very slim and six feet and four inches tall. Doing the wave made him look like those air powered, waving stick men from the old earth.

It turned out that Brandon could literally create waves. Brandon watched Sophie, Chloe and Iksha look for suitable space. They didn't want to go above the castle because that was the direction of the forge. The didn't want to be near the lakes because they used that water for drinking and swimming and the birds droppings would make it dirty.

Brandon was standing near the edge of shelf, wondering what would be a good place for Chloe's birds when he moved his arms in a wave. The ground below the shelf also moved.

Did I do that? Surprised and a little delighted, he looked around. Of course, the other residents felt the tremor and came running out of the castle. "It's OK" Brandon said. "It was just a little wave. "

"What do you mean a little wave?" His stepfather asked.

Sophie stepped in. "Brandon, sweetie, tell me what happened." Brandon told her what he thought had happened. Before Brandon's step dad could scold him, Sophie said, pointedly, "That's is wonderful! Can you move only one section, without shaking the whole mountain?"

"I can try..." Brandon said, nervously glancing at his Step dad.

Sophie nodded to an area across from the stables. "Could you bring up additional land there?" She explained that the other horses would be back by winter and she needed space for another stable.

"Oh, yeah... I think I can do that. How do you want it? I mean... just dirt or rocks also?"

"I believe that a rock foundation, covered with dirt would be safer. What do you think?" Sophie walked the boy through the process of pondering the problem and thinking the solution. "We need something solid, so that rains do not erode it away. It should be an area about four times bigger than the stable, so that we can have room for additional horses..."

As Sophie described the area, in a calm quiet voice, Brandon envisioned the area. He closed his eyes and imagined a rock formation, coming up from the earth, separate from the others. In his mind, he saw the earth surface separate, as if a giant knife had sliced it like a cake. He saw the earth beneath fold and push upward. Slowly, it raised until it was level with the shelf.

Brandon opened his eyes and his knees buckled. Josh held him up with one arm. "Are you all right man?" he asked his friend, laughing. Right before them, stood additional ground. They had only felt a slight tremor. Brandon glowed with happiness.

Sophie nodded and said to Iksha and Chloe: "I believe Brandon can help you raise a portion of land, below the orchard. That should be close enough so that Chloe doesn't have to go far but far enough from Iksha's garden.

"I will talk to my birds and ask them to stay to that area." Chloe said.

Sophie send Brandon to the kitchen and instructed Nick to feed him and tell him about drawing energy from the environment. The best way for a person to reaffirm knowledge, is to teach. As Nick shared with Brandon what he had learned, he would solidify his own knowledge. Together they would explore the principles and, perhaps, discover more.

The more people developed their abilities, the more the others learned to trust their intuition. All except Melissa. She was the eldest of three sisters. She had been an only child, until her mother remarried and had Chloe and Zoe.

Melissa loved her sisters but resented having to share with them. She was a loving girl who loved to help people, however, her self-talk was negative. Apparently, she was afraid to have anything because she thought her parents would take it away. Finances had been tight and Melissa had learned to live with the words "We can't do that."

In reality, Melissa had learned to suck energy from the others by drawing attention to herself. She denied her abilities so that people would reassure her. Josh found her irritating and Sophie could see why. He didn't want to be near her.

"Mom, there is this girl, Melissa... I.. hate to have her around... she drains me." Josh told his Mom.

Sophie nodded. "Uhum... I noticed how the first words out of her mouth are either 'no' or 'can't' I can work with her but it may take a lot of my time."

"Every time we try to teach her something, she finds a reason why she can't do it." Josh said. "...and she interrupts so much..." he added.

"I am not sure that it would be a good thing to force her to listen, like with Nick. That was a desperate situation. The boy was going to hurt himself, if I didn't do something. I know that Melissa will eventually learn... but, in the meantime, she is going to be a pain..." Sophie concluded.

The solution came unexpectedly in the shape of a baby goat. One of Iksha's nannies had given birth to a weak kid. Melissa's heart went to the little guy and she asked Richard and Sophie if they could help him. Richard had been a general practitioner in old earth.

"We could try to feed him and keep an eye on him but there is not much more we can do." he said.

Melissa turned to Sophie and said, "You can heal him... you can do anything." Sophie thought for a moment. She had practiced reconstituting tissue and clearing infection. This little goat, however, had an issue of desire. "Melissa, the goat must want to live in order for any healing to work." Sophie said then, she looked into the girl's eyes and repeated Melissa's favorite words. "I can't."

Melissa could not believe that they were just going to let the little guy die. She refused to accept that nothing could be done. She stayed by the kid's side and fed him herself. She carried the little goat everywhere she went. Her attention was consumed by his welfare. So powerful was her desire to see him thrive that she communicated that desire to him. The little goat bonded with Melissa and slowly, began to respond to her affection.

The days had become hot so one day she took the kid to the lake, where it was cool. She sat under a tree and the sound of rushing water lulled her to sleep. They slept cozy together until the kid got hungry.

Melissa had been feeding him on a schedule and his little stomach noticed the missed meal. He shifted in her arms and found her hand. Melissa woke up to the kid sucking on her thumb. She felt overcome with joy and promptly returned to the castle.

She got milk from the kitchen and with Iksha, watched the little guy slurp the cup clean. The little goat grew stronger every day. It was clear that he would stay by his mistress. Eventually, Iksha and Melissa shared their love for the plants, animals and husbandry chores.

Sophie watched her blossom from the sidelines. She liked that the girl had not given up on hope. Sophie thought about children and what she had learned through her son. Every child had something that captured his or her attention. Some children immediately loved construction machines, while others loved toy race cars. Granted, parental influence had much to do with the choice of toys that a child received, nevertheless, many parents had seen how their kids preferred the box, over the toy that came in it.

Every child also had something that came easy to them. Some painted and drew, some were more physical while others sang and talked a lot. In this world, those interests would translate to the type of vibration that they would be able to manipulate. Singing and talking has to do with anything related to sound. Painting and drawing has to do with creating through visualization and being physical translated to being able to create through manipulation.

Basically, some could say what they wanted, after the idea had formed in their minds. These were the ones who had to study a material or model. The ones who created through manipulation, needed to touch the material then, allow their minds to take over. The ones who drew, would visualize in their minds the item coming together. *That is why we encouraged children to explore art...* Sophie thought to herself.

Josh began everyday, in the castle by going down to the kitchen to start the fires. Sophie and Iksha joined him shortly to begin preparing breakfast. Rachel, Nick's mom, took over for Sophie and joined them in the morning breakfast chores, so Sophie took cleaning chores by visualizing all the dust in the castle being collected into the compost pile. Finally, Melissa took over milking the goats.

Most of the members of the household had picked something they liked to do. They got up early because they had a passion. Every day was a chance to enjoy their work. How different from old earth, where people had to drag themselves out of bed.

Not everyone was happy. There was Allina, Brandon's mother. She had been an inspector in old earth. She did not seem to be able to find her path. Her negative talk hampered her progress. She was not only negative about herself but about her sons, husband and daughter.

When Allina spoke about her family, it was to rehash some issue from the past. She pointed out what they did wrong, instead of focusing on what they did right. Sophie and even Nan, tried to help her but her vacant eyes told them that there was too much noise in her mind.

Allina missed her old routine, her church. She missed sermons. She missed going to church on Sunday and listening to the sermon. There was something in her psyche or ego that blocked her from being able to hear either Sophie or Nan. Her husband, however, found that he loved to work with the horses. He loved the smaller tan ponies Ulrich and his party had ridden and he adored the giant blacks. In return, even though, horses are naturally skittish animals, they trusted this man.

Aside from the castle residents keeping her busy, Sophie continued to keep watch over the grounds. Josh gave her daily reports on the comings and going of the marauders. It seems that the group they met had split into two groups. One group feared the newcomers, while the other group wanted to challenge them.

The group who feared them, believed that the newcomers were either aliens from another planet or Gods. Either way, they reasoned that it was better to befriend them than to antagonize them. They called themselves the believers and began to offer tribute at the foot of the snake.

Sophie often remembered the first day they noticed the practice. Josh and his friends had watched as a tremulous old man approached the snake with flowers and fruit. Josh had been of half a mind to play a trick on the man but he hadn't wanted to scare the poor guy into a heart attack. He waited until the man had stepped back and he vibrated the stones so that the snake glowed. Of course, the flowers and food ignited and disappeared. Finally, Josh molded a smile into the snake's face to show that he had been pleased.

Josh and his friends could barely contain their laughter when Sophie walked in on them. *These kids look like they are having too much fun.* "What are you guys up to?" She asked.

Barely able to contain his amusement, Josh told her about the little old man. He related how he had waited, until the man was at a safe distance, then showed a gesture of good will. He actually felt proud of his restraint.

Sophie turned her eyes to heaven and asked. "Why." she then turned to Josh. "Sweetie... do you have any idea of what you have just done?"

Josh really didn't.

"Josh, you have just begun a new religion." Sophie sighed. *As if I don't have enough to keep me busy already...* "You are going to set up a schedule and come here to listen to their pleas for help. Figure out a way to communicate that to them... and stick to your word." she finally told him.

Josh, still grinning, said "That's OK Mom. I think it will be a good thing. We can establish communication and help them that way."

Sophie reconsidered. "You know what... don't communicate anything to them. Let's just watch them for a while." she instructed, giving him a stern look.

Sophie walked away, shaking her head. These were the moments when she wished that Ulrich would come back. She wasn't sure what he would had done differently but, at least, he would be there to comfort her. She so missed him. In her heart, she felt him alive but it was not enough. It had been three months since he left and she had not dreamed with him. She hadn't had any dreams, that she could remember.

15

ULRICH'S FALL

They found him by the lake. Josh and his friends had been riding about the mountain most of the day. Even though they could fly, they preferred to ride. There was something about riding on a horse with the dogs running about that lent itself for a more personal experience.

It was a hot summer afternoon and the ride had been a workout. They had considered taking a swim in the lake, when they heard distant rumble. Nick, and his brother Michael, thought that it may rain.

Josh looked up at the sky. It was clear. "I think it will be all right. Let's go by the lake anyway." he said.

He laid on a rock, unconscious. Karen, another one of the teenagers, spotted him and called Josh. As they approached the body, Joshua's heart did a somersault. He jumped off his horse and ran to him. "Ulrich!" silently, he prayed that the man would be alive. Ulrich was alive but badly beaten. It was as if this man had fallen from the highest waterfall and bounced off the rocks on his way down.

He opened his eyes and said, "Hey Josh... where's your Mom?" then he fainted.

"MOM!" Josh called.

Sophie's attention had already been drawn to the forest so, when Joshua's call came, she transported to his side immediately. There was her son, beside a bloodied Ulrich. Sophie fell to her knees. She held back emotion and closed her eyes. With her mind, she surveyed the damage.

There was no internal organ damage but a lot of bruises and broken bones. Gently, she floated him back to the castle. Teenagers ran ahead and alerted the castle residents. Iksha waited at the door. Tamara, had placed thick beddings on a long table in the main hall, so Sophie carefully positioned him on top of them.

Iksha and Emily, Karen's mother, began to clean him. Gently, they peeled his clothes off and little by little stripped him bare. He was a mass of cuts, bloodied bruises and swollen, deformed areas.

Sophie indicated the location of the fractures, although they were pretty obvious, and marveled that this man did not have internal injuries. Richard came in and, through Sophie, saw the injuries. His training took over and his ability blossomed.

Iksha saw that Ulrich was very weak so, she instructed the ladies on how to send healing light to Ulrich. "Close your eyes and visualize him in your mind. Take those feelings of concern, that you have, and turn them into love. Find love and hope in your hearts. See the love as a light that flows out of your chest and into Ulrich. Feel the energy flowing from you to him. Do this, as long as you feel good doing it. The moment your attention wanders or you feel tired, stop and take a break. Go get some water or a bite to eat. When you have replenished yourselves, if you like, come back and repeat the process. This may take some time."

Karen and Emily did as instructed. Soon, all three of them glowed. Light healing flowed from them to Ulrich. Sophie felt gratitude.

They worked on him for hours. Richard's abilities developed to the point that he was able to see his patient's injuries on his own. However, he still needed Sophie to guide him in the repair process. Their attention was focused on Ulrich to such a degree, that they also provided him with healing energy.

Josh had joined them. He quickly understood what was going on and joined in the giving. His attention was not fully focused yet so, through the corner of his eye, he noticed movement on the other end of the hall. The rest of the household had gathered and waited. From their perspective, it looked like a group of people staring at Ulrich's body.

Nick made a quick motion to Josh, asking him to come over. Josh, did not know that the newcomers could not see auras yet. He quietly stood up and went to check to see what they needed.

"What are they doing? Is he... dead?" he whispered.

Josh repressed a smile and discreetly explained to them, the best he could, the process of energy healing.

"We should be quiet... " he said after he had finished. He considered telling them that their intentions could also interfere with the process but he decided that it was better to avoid planting the seed of doubt in their minds.

"He is going to be Ok. You guys can sit here, if you like, but this is going to take a long time. I'm here for my Mom. Honestly, I could use some food... Iksha is going to be busy here and..." he hoped to distract them.

Tracy, Chloe's mother and Alina immediately offered to make something to eat. They loved the opportunity to experience Iksha's kitchen. Michael, Nana and Melissa were much more intuitive. Melissa had learned about the power of love and knew what they were doing. Michael and Melissa said that they would stay and watch. Nana went to join Iksha's group.

Edgardo and the others said that they would check in on his progress later. The men where not ready to sit and stare at anything. They preferred to guard the entrances to the castle. Chul-Moo had built a gate from the upper lake to the forge cave. He said he wished to make sure that it was locked. Justin, the ex-soldier, John, his father, and Tom, Karen's father, went to guard the main entrance.

It was night time when Sophie and Richard finished working on Ulrich. They decided to leave him in the hall. Even though it was warm outside, the castle stayed cool so, they covered him with blankets and Sophie sat by his side. Iksha, the ladies and the doctor were exhausted. They decided to grab a bite to eat and go straight to bed. The doctor advised Sophie to get some sleep.

"There is not much more than can be done, Sophie. You should get some rest." he said to her.

"I'll be Ok." stubborn, Sophie stayed by his side all night, with the Termite holding guard over them.

When he woke up in the early morning, Ulrich found that he could barely talk. The broken bones had been mended and the tissue repaired. The blood in his bruises had been dissolved and reconstituted. However, he was still very weak and sore. He looked around and found himself alone. Laying on the table, he recognized the ceiling. This was home. *Sophie should be around somewhere...*

Sophie had stepped to the kitchen, momentarily, and was returning with broth. She gave him broth because she did not know if he could eat food yet. Even his teeth had needed mending.

"Thank you..." he said, finally able to talk. He then added. "Do you have something more solid?"

Sophie felt life come back to her. "I think we can manage." she said with a big smile.

Ulrich got up slowly, carefully testing his joints. "That was something..." he said, referring to the fall. He turned to look at her and smiled. There was happiness but also concern in his look. "How long has it been?" he asked.

"You have been gone... about three months." she informed him.

He nodded. It wasn't that bad considering how much more quickly time passes on earth when compared to the higher realms. He had spent less than two days in the ether. He had not been able to accomplish all he had wanted but at least he had information about the souls who had landed on earth. *That will have to do for now.*

"I heard you." he said.

Sophie frowned. *Which one, of the many times that I thought about him, did he hear?*

"I understand that Josh has started a new religion?" he grinned.

Sophie shook her head as if saying, don't get me started. "Yeah... that." she said.

She really wanted to ask him about his trip but Ulrich nodded and said that they would talk. Right now, he was hungry and wanted to get something to eat. Even though he could draw energy from the environment, this trip had taken all the energy he had and then some. She helped him to the kitchen. Iksha kept a pot of stew at all times, so she served him a bowl with rice. They were sitting at the table when Josh came into the room.

"Hey... Ulrich. How are you feeling?" Josh said, happy to see him up.

"I'm good Josh. You?" Ulrich said with a glint in his eyes.

He would have loved to tease Josh about the snake but he had a feeling that Sophie would not have appreciated that. He was still dazed from the return trip, however, he could tell that she was tense. They barely had time to tell him a little about the newcomers when Richard, Karen, Emily, Iksha, Edgardo and Chul-Moo poured into the room.

"You are awake. Good to have you back my friend!" Edgardo greeted him.

Richard took over and inspected his patient. The bruises had healed nicely and the bones felt sound. Still, he instructed his patient to rest for a while. Get some sleep sir. Richard turned to Sophie and Edgardo. "We should find a bed for him." There were no rooms left. The newcomers had filled the castle.

There was a pause, during which Ulrich stared at Sophie until she, quickly glanced at Josh, then said: "He can come into my room, Richard."

Richard, focused on his patient, did not notice the pause. "Very well then. Let's get him up to your room. Can you walk?" he asked Ulrich.

"I can manage doctor. Thank you." he said, shaking the man's hand to let him know that he appreciated all he had done for him.

Ulrich turned to Josh. "Help me to your Mom's room, Son." Josh put one of Ulrich's arms around his neck and wrapped his own arm around Ulrich's waist. He helped him up then said, "Let's go old man." Sophie turned to Iksha and Emily. The weariness of the night's vigil and months of anxiety came crashing down on her. She looked tired.

Iksha took charge. "Sophie, you also go get some rest, dear. We will take care of things around here. Josh will help us keep watch on the grounds. Later, when you and Ulrich have rested, you can decide how you are going to share the burden. Now go rest."

Josh helped Ulrich up the stairs. Sophie followed behind. Once he had placed Ulrich on her bed, Josh turned to his mom. "Call me if you need anything."

Sophie thanked and hugged her son. She turned to Ulrich. The man was already asleep. She smiled and decided that she needed to take a long, hot bath. Later, she laid down beside him and fell asleep staring at his profile.

They slept for two days. Richard, Josh, Iksha and even Edgardo dropped by, periodically, to check on them. It was as if they had fallen into a coma. Richard could not find anything wrong with them, other than they were unconscious. Josh had an idea that they were traveling but he wasn't sure. They would have to wait.

Sophie opened her eyes and there was a membrane made of colorful strings. The whole room was made of strands of gauze with crisscrossed bright red, purple and yellow strings. Pleasant diffuse light bounced off some of the sheets of gauze and illuminated others form behind. She sensed him and turned around. Ulrich was coming to her. He also looked confused.

"We are we, Ulrich?" she asked him.

"I don't know Sophie. I know that we are not in the seventh. I... we can't go back there." he said.

Sophie remembered the last time she had been in the seventh. They had not been exactly nice to her. "I don't believe that I mind that too much." she said.

Ulrich looked at her. She did not understand yet, he thought.

"Anyway... we are here. You might as well tell me about your trip. What happened?" Sophie asked.

He took her by the hand and invited her to sit on a soft surface, that had gently bubbled from the floor. "I... The other souls, the ones who became aware through me, went to different worlds. Many came to our earth but many more fell on third dimension earth. They had tried to follow me but they got confused because third dimension earth still existed. I am not sure that it will ever cease to exist."

"It won't." a beautiful woman said. She stood in front of them, as if she had been part of the conversation all along.

"Hi." Sophie said. "You look familiar."

"Yes, I am Mirinus. You could call me one of your angels." she smiled.

Mirinus shook her curly bob and casually pulled the right side behind her ear. She had a fantastic smile and beautiful skin that glowed. Her outfit was conservative but too stylish for Sophie's idea of an angel. Sophie raised an eyebrow, slightly.

"Where are we?" she asked.

"We are at the crosswise. One of the crosswises. This... is a moment in time. We can see what all the intersecting dimensions have done, in this point. We jump from crosswise to crosswise to study other moments in time." Mirinus answered, as if she were discussing geometry.

"Could we call this... 'The Time Dimension'?" Sophie asked.

"Not the whole of it. Just one point. However, this point contains all of creation, at this moment in time." Mirinus explained. She then turned to Ulrich. "It worries you that you are not welcome on the seventh. You are, however, very welcome here." she smiled at him.

"Why does this dimension exist?" Sophie asked.

Mirinus raised an eyebrow. "My... you do ask loaded questions... " she sat in front of them and rested her elbows on her knees. "What happens when one organization has complete control without checks and balances?" she whispered.

"Absolute power corrupts absolutely..." Sophie remembered a saying from her days in the military.

"Correct. Right now, humans believe that the structure is like a ladder... lower dimensions, middle of the road and then higher and ascended. In reality, somebody is always watching the watchers." she said with a dazzling smile.

"What is going to happen on earth?" Ulrich asked.

Mirinus nodded. "You mean this earth? It is all very fluid right now... Some souls will seek you... to lead them... Others want to learn more from you. Oh, they are incredibly gifted but they have forgotten what it is to be human. Unlike you, most of them were ascended with their twin, when they became aware. ...and then there is the group that will fall into... fear and anger. You can't help it. It always happens..."

"Always happens?" Sophie raised an eyebrow.

Mirinus smiled and cocked her head. "Seriously? You really do not remember?"

Sophie felt confused then, she remembered. "The cycle of creation and destruction. Through these dimensions, you can see the whole cycle."

Mirinus nodded approval. "Some people call us time travelers." then she winked and was gone.

Even after all that she had been through, Sophie found it disconcerting to see someone appear and disappear. She turned to Ulrich but he was also gone. Sophie found herself alone. At first, she felt apprehension then, she remembered where she was. "I want to see Ulrich's fall."

Immediately she was in the middle of an incredible space. It looked like a huge cavern and there were eyes on the walls. The walls pulsated and flowed. *Eew...* she thought, then she saw Ulrich running. Men were chasing him. They wanted to grab him to do something to him. She felt that their touch would hurt him. A small slit opened in between two of the eyes and Ulrich dove into it.

The scene changed. She saw the earth, space, then the sky and far below, the shelf. Ulrich was falling inside a bubble. The bubble began to burn. Ulrich looked like he was trying to stop it but he was going too fast. He hit the ground and bounced. Momentum carried him forward and he bounced off the rocks, until, he landed where they found him. Shaken, Sophie said aloud. "I have seen enough. I want to go back."

She fell into her body and opened her eyes. Ulrich was not in the bed. She heard sounds coming from the bathroom. It was him. Sophie stared at the ceiling and went through the images that she had just seen. *Dear God... it is a miracle that he is alive.* Sophie sat up in the bed and saw Ulrich come out of the bathroom. He had a towel wrapped around his waist. Faint lines and smudges, tenuously shined on his muscular torso and arms.

"Hallo." he said and stood there, looking at her for a moment. He came and sat at the edge of the bed. He could tell that she was shaken. "You saw?" he asked.

Sophie nodded. "What did they want to do to you?" she asked.

Ulrich nodded. "I am not sure. They wanted to touch me... to count me or something to do with records."

A chill went through her body. "Ulrich... can those beings... never mind. I don't want to think about that right now." she shook her head and hugged him.

Ulrich held her tight for a long time, then he kissed her. When he released her, Sophie moved back into the bed and laid down invitingly. Ulrich shook his head.

Sophie raised an eyebrow.

Ulrich laughed and finally said. "There's work to do."

Now she was truly confused. "What? Get out. Do you feel OK now? If so, get out." She got up to go to the bathroom. "...tease..." she muttered under her breath.

Ulrich caught up with her. Still smiling, he said, "I have a surprise for you." Ulrich wouldn't tell her anymore. He got dressed and went to find the others. Sophie finished her morning ritual and went to search for Iksha. She had an idea about what Ulrich meant but she wanted to be cautious. *Any way you see it... this brother sun and sister moon situation is getting old...* she told herself on the way to the kitchen.

16

THERE IS GOING TO BE A WEDDING

It was strange to see so many new faces. Ulrich felt a like a visitor, instead of the builder. Specially when he saw the new details in the castle. There were seat cushions on the chairs in the main hall and additional carvings on the walls.

Edgardo has been busy... and Tamara has become very good at weaving, he thought as he walked down the hallway and through the main hall.

He found Iksha in the kitchen and called her aside.

"Hello dear. It is good to have you back." Iksha beamed at him.

"Thank you... Iksha, have you been able to prepare things? I know it is a lot to ask of you..." he began to ask her.

"Certainly dear. It is not a problem. Tamara is also helping me. We each have our responsibilities but Sophie has everything. She has to know how to do everything, teach everyone and keep an eye on everyone. I am glad that you are here. You can help her now. We are still planning for the longest day of the summer. You made it back on time. That was good of you." Iksha rambled.

Ulrich grinned and hugged her warmly. "Thank you Iksha." he said. He left Iksha and went looking for Edgardo and Chul-Moo. He felt that they would be somewhere in the caves. On the way there, he ran into Josh.

"Hey... Ulrich. How are you doing?" Josh said. He had been experimenting with light. The darkness of the cave offered him the perfect environment.

"Josh." Ulrich nodded. He watched as the boy created little sparklers and beams. "That is very good... This is a good place too. If you were to do this outside, the light would be seen for miles. Promise that you won't do this outside. It really is not a good time to have to deal with the locals. By the way, I'm looking for Chul-Moo and Edgardo. Are they upstairs?"

"Uhum." Joshua nodded and continued his mini-light show.

While Ulrich was looking for Edgardo and Chul-Moo, Sophie had made it to the kitchen. The kitchen, as usual, smelled wonderful. Iksha was busy moving from the grill to the work table and back to the grill. There were platters with sautéed vegetables, rice and chicken awaiting hungry mouths.

"Hello dear! Ulrich was just here." Iksha beamed at Sophie.

"Yes..." She had a hunch that Iksha might know what Ulrich planned. She decided to test her theory. "Has Ulrich asked you about the preparations?"

"Yes dear! It will be a wonderful celebration. The longest day of the year and we will say our vows! Has Tamara fitted you yet?" Iksha asked.

Sophie, leaned on the table and, discreetly, sat down on the nearest chair. Her mind reeled. *Dress... vows...celebration?* What was Iksha talking about? The summer solstice had been a pagan celebration.

"No." she finally said, truthfully. "Has she... yours?" she asked, fishing for more information.

"No. Now that you mention it... I have to check with her. She may have been too busy with the newcomers." Iksha reasoned aloud then she said. "Zoe. Go get Tamara, child. Hurry!"

Alina, Emily and several of the other females had been listening to the exchange. Alina could not contain her curiosity and asked. "What celebration?"

"We are getting married, of course!" Iksha said.

The females looked from her to Sophie. "Who is getting married to whom?" Karen asked.

Impatient, Iksha said "Child... I am getting married to Edgardo and Sophie is getting married to Ulrich, of course!"

There was a split second of silence, then congratulations exploded. The conversation became a blur of female voices. Tamara walked into the room and they rushed her. Everybody wanted to see the dresses and asked what they could do to help.

Sophie sat at table, with her chin on her hand. She smiled and nodded at the expressions of affection and enthusiasm. Her heart had stopped, for what felt like a very long time, restarted with a jolt and now it was at full gallop. She was actually holding her chin to keep it from shaking.

Sophie didn't know if to feel happy, furious or terrified. Ulrich had planned her wedding without checking with her. *...or did he...* She could remember the people in the screen room. She remember him but she did not remember having any conversations about a wedding. When she found her voice, Sophie thanked Iksha and made some excuse about remembering something.

Upstairs, at the forge, Ulrich ran into Justin and the other men. They were observing how Chul-Moo worked the iron. Chul-Moo and the men nodded recognition at Ulrich. Now that Ulrich was here, Chul-Moo began to tell them about how Josh had created the fire that never goes out.

"I don't know how he does it. This fire never goes out and it burns hot... really hot." he said.

The men looked at each other. It was difficult for them to believe their eyes. Chul-Moo had been fashioning spear heads for them.

"Why are you making spears?" Ulrich asked.

The men turned surprised then, remembered that Ulrich had not been there when they first arrived. They told him the story of their rescue and how they had decided to arm themselves. They already had bows. Ulrich was about to ask them what other plans they had, when, Edgardo came in.

"Ulrich. Good thing I find you here. I have the stones." he said.

Ulrich turned his attention to the pouch on Edgardo's hand. There were precious stones Edgardo had mined from new branches of the cave. Ulrich nodded appreciatively. "Care to switch?" Ulrich asked Chul-Moo.

With a wide grin the other man agreed. The other men asked what was going on and Edgardo filled them in about the upcoming celebration.

"Whoa... we have a wedding. When is this supposed to happen?" Tom asked.

Ulrich and Edgardo looked at each other. It was not easy to tell time. It had been early summer when they first arrived and Ulrich had been away for almost three months. It should be June already.

"I would say that in less than five days. Have you been keeping track of the sunset?" Ulrich asked Edgardo.

"Yes. I have the dial on top of the roof. The days are longer." answered the other man.

"What are you talking about, man?" Justin asked.

"We will celebrate on the longest day of the year." Edgardo explained to the men. "We do not have calendars here so, I had to measure the time it took for the sun to set, everyday, since we have been here."

"Whatever. That calls for a celebration. Too bad we do not have beer." Justin said, shrugging his shoulders.

"Ho..ho... but we do..." said Chul-Moo. "Let's finish here and we will show you." Chul-Moo went to work. After about an hour, he presented the rings. The men regarded them. There was something striking about such beauty glistening in the dirty forge. Ulrich held his set in the palm of his hand. He took a deep breath and nodded. The men remembered the beer so, Edgardo took them to the cellars.

On their way back, they ran into Josh. All the men, except Ulrich gave him wide smiles and patted him on the back. Josh was about to ask if he had won something, when he caught Ulrich's eyes. He raised an eyebrow. "Don't tell me..." he said to the man.

The men left them behind, in a hurry to get to the beer. Instead of telling him, Ulrich produced the rings and showed them to Josh. The boy nodded and said. "Ok..." He then stared at Ulrich. Before he could say anything, Ulrich told him that he had spoken with Sophie about Sabrina. Josh didn't know what to say. His mother had not mentioned anything but he liked Ulrich and if he made his mother happy he was Ok with it.

"Ok, then... when is the celebration?" he asked.

"In about five days. I want to celebrate on summer solstice." Ulrich said.

Josh raised an eyebrow. "Summer solstice? Wasn't that a pagan celebration?"

Ulrich laughed and shook his head. "Actually, it began as a farmer's celebration. Long summer days allowed for more opportunity to grow food. I thought it would be the perfect day because of the weather and longer light... easy to remember."

"Yeah... some people may not agree." Josh grinned.

Ulrich also grinned and said: "That... coming from the new God of Schloss Am See?"

"Aw..." Josh groaned and laughed good naturedly. "I... was just having fun with the guys."

"It's Ok Son. We'll think of something... about how to handle those people." Ulrich patted him on the shoulder. He asked Josh if he was coming or staying. Josh wanted to practice a little more, so Ulrich left and went in search of Sophie.

Excited female voices could be heard all the way into the first cave. Ulrich turned into the hallway to the kitchen and wondered, amused, what could have them so excited. His heart sank... they knew somehow. Sophie knew. He should have asked her but he wanted to have the rings first.

He braced himself and stepped into the kitchen. Silence happened. Everybody looked at him with poorly concealed excitement. He didn't see Iksha so he nodded to the group and quickly found his way through.

17

SOPHIE REMEMBERS

Sophie was by the lake. She had felt the need to get away from everyone to think in silence. The castle bustled with people and she hardly ever had a moment to herself anymore. Sophie wanted to find her emotions. What did she truly feel... excitement, happiness or fear? Check on all three.

Sophie wanted to cry, laugh and take off running, all at the same time. She took a deep breath and decided to study the facts. Ulrich told her this morning that he had a surprise for her. She tricked the information out of Iksha. He was Joshua's father. He had kept a secret from her before... make that two. She did not remember talking about a wedding with him. She remembered his touch, kiss, eyes... basically she remembered him.

"He is not yours..." Sophie snapped to attention. She had heard a voice nearby. There was a new presence, different from that of the forest creatures. "Show yourself." she said. Her mirror image on the lake began to raise out of the water. As the image began to take shape, Sophie stood up and stepped back. Mirror Sophie stepped out of the lake and stood on the shore, smiling obscenely to her.

"Who are you?" Sophie asked.

"Isn't it obvious? I am you, dear." the image said.

"No, it is not obvious... you look like me but you are not me." Sophie stood her ground.

"He didn't think so. He loved me, you know. Sometimes, he misses me... I am a lot more fun. You are too serious and worried all the time. Let's just say that he liked me better." the image smiled, satisfied.

"He is not with you." Sophie retorted then realized that the image had engaged her in conversation. *That's what evil does. It gets our attention and makes us focus on it. Evil wants attention to drain our energy.* Sophie grinned. "You poor thing..." she turned to leave when the image changed slightly.

It was not mirror Sophie anymore but Sabrina. She did look a lot like Sophie; they could have been sisters. She felt a pang of guilt then reminded herself that evil is a trickster. *Evil will resort to anything in order to get our attention.* She looked at Sabrina with a smidgen of pity then said: "I am sorry about the choice that you made. I am sorry that you have chosen to cling to this world. However, it has been your choice." Again, she turned to walk away.

The voice came back a little higher but still taunting: "I wonder what that beautiful son of yours is doing? Oh... he is in the cave... tsk, tsk, accidents happen."

Sophie swirled around and with everything she had in her heart she yelled. "I am done with you. GO TO HELL!" Her anger exploded into pure light. Sabrina had a split second to realize her mistake. Thunderstorm clouds gathered, lightning crackled, the earth shook and Sabrina was hit dead center.

Vaporized; only a burn mark remained to prove that she had been there.

Her anger spent, Sophie scanned the land. Her son was Ok; just a little surprised. There were a couple of broken dishes in the kitchen and commotion but the residents were uninjured. Ulrich was... She turned around. Ulrich stood staring at her with something like green fire in his eyes.

He nodded slowly. "Do you remember now?" he asked.

Sophie inhaled deeply. "I remember." she said simply. She walked to him and took him by the hand. This time it was her who said: "Let's walk."

They walked in silence, holding hands and taking deep breaths. Each breath helped them release negative energy. They reached the shelf and, within seconds, the castle residents poured out in confusion.

"Did Brandon do something again?" Yelled his step dad.

"How could I? I was standing right beside you, remember?" Brandon yelled back.

Sophie raised a hand to quiet the crowd. "It was not Brandon."

Ulrich stood and addressed the crowd. "It was none of you. There was a threat and it has been vanished. You are all safe."

There was more talk and confusion. Of course, the residents wanted to know what had been the nature of the threat and who had vanished it. Then they wanted to know how it had been vanished. Ulrich and Sophie answered their questions without giving away details from the past.

Eventually, the residents left with the idea that a corrupt being had attacked Sophie and that she had defended herself. Justin listened but didn't say much. He called the other men to join him back in the cellars. Eventually, everyone resumed their interrupted activities.

Josh turned to Ulrich. "I know what you mean now."

Josh had been in the cave when he thought of his mom. In his mind, he saw her swirl and throw something like pure light at something, then the earthquake happened. He had immediately left the cave, quickly made his way through the castle and joined the group, during the middle of the explanations.

"Who... what happened?" he asked his Mom.

Sophie looked at him for a minute. "There was an angry spirit who wanted to hurt us and... I took care of it."

Josh shook his head. "I think that was more dramatic than my little snake. I'm sure that was felt all the way to the marauder camp."

Sophie simply nodded her head. "Uhum. Let's hope they don't associate it with us."

Josh sighed deeply and said: "Too late. You had a witness Mom. There was a scout around the area. I don't believe he's going to stop running until tomorrow." he grinned.

In spite of herself, Sophie laughed. "Oh... my goodness. This is not funny."

That night, Sophie was unusually absentminded and the residents were unusually talkative. Everybody recounted their experience and impressions of the earthquake. Ulrich and Josh stole quick, amused glances at her. Sophie just smiled and shook her head.

When the conversation switched to the wedding, Sophie wished she could come up with a plausible excuse to leave. Everybody discussed the plans for the celebration. The thing became an entity on it's own. Sophie resigned herself to be a guest at her own wedding. She nodded and agreed or referred them to Ulrich or Iksha.

Just tell me what to wear and point me to where I am supposed to be and let's get it over with... she said to herself.

Ulrich squeezed her hand, from time to time, while he carried on conversations with the residents. Iksha and Tamara were on a roll. They designed and decided the dresses. Men and women would have new outfits. They created a weaving circle and the other women were going to learn and help.

Finally, the night was over. Sophie turned to Josh. "Stay in the castle at night, please. Ok?" Josh promised he would. She turned to Ulrich and kissed him lightly. "I'm going to bed." she said. Ulrich needed to discuss something with Chul-Moo and the men, then he would join her.

Sophie soaked in the bathtub and thought about all that had happened. There had been an angry spirit in *this* world. She had not expected those to exist in this world. In addition, she wondered how would the marauder scout describe what he saw? She shook her head, *It is amazing how these situations have a way of getting out of hand.*

She dressed in summer sleep shorts and top. *Tamara has been busy*, she thought, and laid on the bed. Sophie was about to doze into sleep, when Ulrich came in and sat beside her. She didn't have the energy to be mad at him. She had just sat through a whole night of her wedding being planned and the groom not having asked her yet. He had a mixture of guilt and amusement dancing in his eyes.

Ulrich knew that this was one of those moments when words are not enough so he simply produced the ring. "I was waiting to have this..." he said as a way of apology.

Sophie looked at the ring then turned her stare to Ulrich. Finally, she extended her arm from under the covers and offered him her hand. Ulrich slid the engagement ring on her finger. It truly was beautiful. Sophie looked at the ring, then back at Ulrich and shook her head as if saying: "This is a crazy situation." They looked at each other for a very long time.

"Thoughts and words become things..." Sophie finally said. "This is... insane..."

Ulrich smiled wryly "A whole planet... full of people with the ability to create their own reality..."

"Ulrich... this world was not supposed to be this way..." she said.

Ulrich nodded and patted her arm. He got up and went to the bathroom to take a shower. There is something intimately comforting about the sound of a shower, while a mate is in there. Sophie laid on her side and looked at the ring. She remembered now. It wasn't like Ulrich had dropped on one knee and asked her to marry him. Souls in the ether have a different language.

Ulrich had been there when she came out of stasis. She had been very confused and asked about Josh constantly. They showed her where Josh laid, still in stasis. Once she saw that her son was safe, she was able to relax a little. She spent a lot of time with Ulrich.

They didn't use words to communicate. They merged and exchanged their energies. She gave him her light and he reflected it back to her. She saw herself in him and he saw himself in her. She had felt complete and happy.

Ulrich came out of the shower. He wore short pajamas without a shirt. Sophie watched him as he walked around the bed and laid down beside her. He reached over and slid one arm under her and pulled her into a cradle. Sophie looked up at him and opened her mouth to speak but he placed his index on her lips. His aura came to her and wrapped her with it's glow.

He ran his index down her chin, neck and over the swell of her breast. Sophie felt a wave of pleasure and looked at him, uncertain. Ulrich gave her the slightest of winks then returned his attention to her body. His touch was light but secure. Slowly, he traced the rise of her nipple and brought it to painful awareness. Sophie loved that initial wave of pleasure as her body became aroused. He lowered his hand and brought it up under her shirt. The touch of his hand, warm against her skin, made her gasp in agreement. He moved his hand behind her back and pushed her closer to him. Sophie pressed herself against him. His lips met hers in a slow exploration of each other. He held her close to him and took possession of her mouth. After a while, Sophie pushed him back for air and Ulrich pulled her shirt off. He looked at her and traced the lines of her shoulders, arms and chest with his hand. He leaned over to kiss her again and moved his hand around to her back. Sophie's body arched, undulated and moaned in agreement. His hand moved from her back to the curve of her hips, down her thighs and legs. His face found the crook of her neck and his lips the nearby lobe. Sophie traced the hard muscles in his arms, the curve of his back, the firmness of his buttocks and the muscles on his thighs. Ulrich moved down her neck to her chest. With one hand he cupped a breast while his tongue traced the circle of the nipple. Arching her body to offer more of herself, she caressed his shoulders and ran her fingers through his hair.

He pushed her shorts off and she felt his hand find the inside of her thighs and the warm moist spot in between her legs. Her body responded and arched closer to him. He pulled his shorts off and rolled on top of her. He felt her breasts push hard against him and the strong beat of her heart. They kissed and caressed each other until he reached down and guided himself to her. She was very moist, warm and engorged. Ulrich's own juices met hers and they both felt a wave of pleasure. He pushed, gently parting her swollen lips, and making room for himself. She closed her eyes and opened herself to him. Her response surprised her. She had not been with a man in years but her body knew him. She came to meet him and in a gasp they were joined. Rocking rhythmically they felt themselves loose all sense of their surroundings. There was nothing but the heat of their bodies, the softness and fullness of their lips and the increasing waves of pleasurable tension in their genitals. He pushed deeper and she raised one of her legs and held him close with it; the other, she used to caress his leg. Ulrich held her close while he felt her inside and outside. She was warm, moist and held him firmly. He raised her other leg and opened her more to him. Sophie gasped at how completely open and bare to him she felt; he filled her completely and she could not hide her pleasure. Their tension increased until it felt like their hearts would explode. Heat flushed from her chest up her face. She gasped and arched her back and he pushed deeper. Their bodies became extremely tense, then release came. They held tight to each other while rhythmic contractions pulsated in waves of pleasure. Spent, they kissed and looked at each other. They stayed like that, in the afterglow, without speaking. Ulrich stayed inside of her and kissed her over and over. He kissed her lips, her face and moved down to her ear.

"I love you." he said.

Sophie held him tightly. She found that she could not speak. She felt as if reality itself had disappeared. Ulrich's glow had gone from red to green to gold. She had seen herself through his eyes. She was beautiful and she glowed. She felt him and she felt herself. It was as if she was herself and him at the same time. She felt what he felt and there were no words to describe it. She closed her eyes and enjoyed the sensation of floating. Slowly, she drifted away into sleep.

Ulrich smiled, kissed her lightly and reluctantly pulled himself off her. He cradled her and watched her sleep, then he pulled the covers over themselves and snuggled up to her.

He had experienced the same overlapping of the senses as she had. However, he had watched and experienced the world through her for so long that it did not come as a surprise. He knew this had been a new and shocking experience for Sophie. He pressed her against him. "It gets better Sophie." he whispered in her ear.

18

RELEASING THE PAST

She woke up in his arms. It was still dark. His body cradled her in warmth and sensuality. She loved the feel of his chest against her back. His thigh rested in between her legs and pushed possessively against her moisture. His hand rested naturally on her breast.

Each one of his breaths send waves of pleasure through her body. Instinctively, she began to caress his arm and shifted her hips. She felt him come back to life. Stretching and inhaling deeply, he buried his lips in her neck and squeezed her breast, then moved his hand down her stomach. He found her moist already and murmured something in her ear. She pushed her hips against him and with one swift movement he pushed her on her back and parted her legs.

He entered her without preamble. She raised to meet his hunger. They pushed and worked themselves into a rhythm. There was no gentleness this time, only hunger. Tension mounted and he felt her become tighter. He knew she was near climax so he pushed deeper and held her tighter. Their whole body contracted and exploded. Slower, they rocked with each subsiding contraction.

Eventually he spoke. "Good morning."

Sophie sighed against his neck. She could stay like that for the rest of her days. With one hand, he grabbed her by the buttocks and with the other he supported her back while he turned them both and laid on his back. She laid on his chest, completely open and joined to him, while Ulrich traced circles on her back. Eventually, her nature got the better of her and she began to giggle. Ulrich looked at her puzzled.

"What's so funny" he asked.

Sophie felt him slip out and the earthiness of the sensation sent her into laughter. "I was beginning to worry... brother sun." she said, repressing her laughter. His knitted brows send her into laughter and she rolled off him.

Ulrich rolled against her and asked: "Who is brother sun?"

Sophie could barely contain her laughter. After a moment she explained that brother sun and sister moon was a reference to an old movie about St. Francis of Assisi and Clare. He found God through chastity and deprivation and Clare, who had been helping the lepers, became his chaste companion.

Ulrich rolled back in laughter. "Is that what you thought we were going to be?"

"I was beginning to wonder..." Sophie said.

Ulrich grinned and shook his head. "Not in this lifetime. Not that I finally have you in the flesh. God never said to deny the nature of our bodies... that was an invention by men who wanted to restrict women's light."

Sophie looked at him surprised. It was the first time that he mentioned God. "What else did God say?" she asked.

"God speaks to us through our hearts. Humans know what is the right thing to do because of the emotion they feel. Every time a person is about to do something that will get them in trouble, there is a feeling of anger, anxiety, fear or apprehension involved. The majority rationalize the action but the internal discomfort remains. That is why they try to convince themselves and others that they are right. That is why they talk so much... they are looking for validation from others. Truth does not need to convince anyone. It does not make excuses and it does not ask for reassurance. Truth just is... " he explained then, a shadow crossed his eyes so he added. "...and we both know that the truth, eventually, comes out."

She looked at him and caressed his face. Sophie felt gratitude. "I love you." she said simply.

He looked at her and caressed her face. He had waited so long to hear those words in the flesh. This life and being with her and Josh meant a lot to him.

She remembered what she had wanted to ask him the night before. "Ulrich, this world was not supposed to be this way. Everything I read said that this would be a perfect society... in harmony."

Ulrich sighed. "Yes. People were told that they only needed to meditate and become spiritual. That they would move into a higher vibration where they would only have to think of something and it would happen. As you can see, there was an ingredient of truth in that. The messengers did not explore the concepts however. Humans have an active imagination. How could anyone, after decades of witnessing evil, forget about it? The memory of evil attracts that vibration."

Sophie felt stunned. "So I attracted Sabrina?"

"In part. Her anger inspired her to cling to this world and your guilt and doubts became a beacon." he said.

"I have to be very careful about what I think..." she said.

Ulrich grinned; he couldn't help himself. "Now you get it."

Sophie grinned back and thumped him. They hugged and kissed for a minute then Ulrich sat up on the bed. He declared himself famished and as much as he would love to stay with her all day, his body needed solid food. "Besides, I want to check on the celebration and the men." he added.

"Yeah... about that... why the solstice?" Sophie asked.

He shrugged it off. "If I had realized that it was going to cause so much controversy, I would have chosen any other day. I just thought that it would be nice to have a special day to mark our vows."

"What about the men?" she asked.

Ulrich stood up and, as he walked to the bathroom, he said. "I believe we have the beginning of a militia. Justin... believes that we detonated a bomb yesterday."

Sophie's eyes grew large and she shook her head. *These things do have a way of getting out of hand.*

The castle had become a community. The upcoming celebration had brought everyone together. There was food to prepare, furniture to move in the main hall, wood to collect for the outside bonfire, clothes to make and a script to create. It was decided that the bride and groom would write their own vows and Nan would preside.

"Well, I have never been a member of the clergy but I have been to enough weddings to remember the words. This is a new world... perhaps we should make it nondenominational." she said.

Sophie nodded in approval. Nan was very intuitive. She understood that people had different beliefs. It was better to avoid separation. Alina did not agree. She had been a regular at Sunday service and believed that she had been saved by the Christian God.

"We have all been saved, Alina." Sophie told her. "We have Buddhists, Muslims, Catholics, Baptists and who knows what else in here... According to the preachers, they should not be here."

Alina didn't miss a step. "God wanted to show them his mercy and he allowed them to come and join us."

Sophie sighed. In old earth, she had never wasted time in these types of debates. *There are more important things in life.* "Ok... well... I prefer a nondenominational ceremony." and she left it at that.

Other than Alina, everyone else was happy with the choice and they busied themselves with the preparations. Sophie and Ulrich took to taking walks after lunch, just so they could get away from the heightened emotional energies in the castle. Coming back from a walk with Ulrich, Sophie noticed Josh standing by the edge of the shelf. She smiled when she saw her son but, when she tuned into him, she detected a note of expectation.

"What is it sweetie?" She asked, coming to stand beside him.

Ulrich, beside her, looked from Josh to the surrounding forests. "We had company today." he said.

"Yep. Again." Josh said turning to his mother. "Your little antennas have been off, huh?" he said grinning.

"Wait... what?" Sophie frowned.

"It's Ok Mom. They're well on their way off the mountain. It was a couple of scouts." Josh said, casually. "I can tell you that there is turmoil among the marauders. We have given them plenty to talk about."

Ulrich gave a stern look to his spiritual son. He had created the perennial nightly fog shroud but he knew that it was not enough. Josh had continued to experiment with light. He had moved from the cave to the lake, where he played by twisting droplets of water from the water falls. He created rainbows of impossible shapes; spirals, squares, bursting flowers, any shape he could imagine.

Ulrich had instructed him to be mindful of his surroundings, before using his abilities in the open. Apparently, Josh had forgotten his advice. Actually, Josh had not forgotten; he just did not believe in hiding. He was certain that a confrontation would happen sooner or later. He preferred to get the issue out of the way.

"As long as we keep on hiding, we will never be able to communicate and help these people." Josh said. Josh felt that the marauders were just people who were scared and hungry. It was the other group of survivors that bothered him.

Sophie could understand both points of view. She agreed with her son, in that they should find a way to communicate with the locals. However, he should have not ignored Ulrich's advice.

"Listen. Mom... I am sorry..." Josh began, then he turned to Ulrich. "I respect you and... forgive me for being rude... you're with my Mom but you are not my father." Josh said evenly.

Now it was Ulrich's turn to look at Sophie. "You haven't told him." he said, amused.

"Told me what?" Josh asked.

Sophie sighed deeply. "How do you explain something like that?" she said, at a loss.

Ulrich smiled and looked at Josh. "Son, brace yourself. We have a story to tell you."

"Wow..." Josh said with arched eyebrows, when they had finished. Then, with a glint in his eyes he said, "It was about time you told me. I had a feeling..."

Sophie and Ulrich looked at Josh dumbfounded. The boy looked unfazed. There was a moment of silence then, Josh asked, "Is it alright if I call you Dad now?" Josh had not been calm. In that moment, Sophie and Ulrich realized just how happy he truly felt. His earth father had never been part of his life. He had buried the sting of rejection deep and told himself that he didn't care.

Ulrich stepped forward and hugged Josh. "I would like that." he said.

Josh had, never in his life, been hugged by another man. At first, he held back but, little by little, years of hoping and waiting in vain for his father to visit him, came to the surface. They hugged for a long time. When they finally separated, with self-conscious smiles, they wiped their tears.

Sophie was in not much better shape. Watching them heal, allowed her to let go off resentment. After a while, in between sniffles, all three looked at each other and laughed. Words were not necessary. Release had made them lighter. They felt connected and happy.

19

THE CELEBRATION

The castle looked and smelled amazing. Iksha had coaxed vines with flowers to grow from pots up and around the pillars in the main hall. The men had cleared the area in front one of the fireplaces, where Ulrich built a decorative arch. The ladies had garlanded flowers together and placed them on the arch and tables.

There was venison and goat meat roasting in an outside pit. A barrel of wine and a barrel of beer had been brought from the cellars. It turned out that Michael could slow down the molecules in water so the barrel of beer sat in a tub of ice. A large pile of wood laid in front of the building, waiting for night time to be ignited. Everybody had worked hard to prepare the castle for the celebration.

The ladies looked beautiful in crimson dresses with small details in gold. Iksha wore a gorgeous sari and Sophie wore a gown, both cream with gold details. The men chose long linen dress tunics with trousers and closed leather shoes. Their clothes were a mixture of old earth East and West influences.

Nan had chosen a purple gown because, according to her, everybody looked good in purple. She presided over the ceremony with warmth and humor. Josh gave away his mother and Richard gave Iksha away. There were no ring bearers so one of the witnesses carried the rings.

It was a simple ceremony where Iksha, Edgardo, Sophie and Ulrich said very similar vows. They promised to respect, honor, love, protect and be kind to another until death. Ulrich added the phrase "to eternity" to his vows. Sophie nodded and understood his meaning.

After the ceremony, Chloe presented them with music through her birds. It was amazing to hear the sounds she and her birds could coax through their vocals chords. There were fast and slow dancing tunes. Everybody was astounded.

Night fell and the party moved outside. That's when the true party began. The pile burned high and the music began. Josh and his friends had fashioned drums, which along with Chloe's high notes, contributed to a very medieval but happy musical background. The residents ate until sated and drank until lightheaded.

Sophie stood by the fire while Ulrich brought her a cup of wine. He tapped his cup to hers and drank in a toast. He stood looking straight into her eyes a moment. Under the light of the flames, his strong features stood out and his eyes shone even more. Sophie thought that she had never met a more handsome man.

He grabbed her by the hand and took her to their spot near the edge of the shelf. In order to have the celebration, he had retreated the fog to the lands below. For a moment, Sophie wondered if the fire could be seen, then she remembered the power of thoughts. She shook her head and chased them away immediately. Instead, she focused on enjoying the scene before her. Her son played music, while the dogs, intent on grabbing leftovers, did their best to avoid getting stepped on by dancers. She turned to Ulrich with a wide grin. "They look very happy" she said.

Ulrich looked at the residents for a minute. He sat down on a boulder and pulled her on his lap. He buried his head in her hair and nuzzled her neck. He took a deep breath, "It is good for them to celebrate. Every year, we will celebrate this day. We have been through many changes..."

"Why do you sound almost worried?" she asked him.

He nodded, "It is not worry... There is more people coming Sophie. Different types of people. We are going to be busy..." then he looked at her and kissed her deeply. "Tonight, we celebrate."

ABOUT THE AUTHORS

Freiderici and Allen Paige are mother and son. They live in Tennessee, where she retired from the U.S. Army. The book is the result of a fun project they began, one night after watching one too many movie about "The End Of The World"

If people spend more time listening to each other and looking for similarities, instead of differences, we might have less problems.

Freiderici wrote the draft chapters, then asked Paige to review them. He pointed mistakes and suggested changes. *The "swirling lava snake" is entirely his but the smile on it, is mine because I could, totally, see him doing something like that.* The love scenes were written entirely by Freiderici without any participation from Paige. *I didn't even want him to read those chapters in the finished book. However, I felt that they needed to be part of the book.*

Paige loves games, to spend time with this friends and anything technology. They do have two dogs, very similar to the ones in the book but with a lot more personality. Freiderici works from home where clients call her for questions about databases and, many times, life advice.

For questions or comments about the book they can be contacted through TalesOfAnew@gmail.com .

Made in the USA
Charleston, SC
13 February 2014